The Seven Autopsies of Nora Hanneman

The Seven Autopsies of Nora Hanneman

stories

Courtney E. Morgan

EC2

TUSCALOOSA

The University of Alabama Press

Tuscaloosa, Alabama 35487-0380

Manufactured in the United States of America

FC2 is an imprint of the University of Alabama Press

Book Design: Publications Unit, Department of English, Illinois State University; Director: Steve Halle; Production Assistant: Chantel Reeder

Cover Design: Lou Robinson

Typeface: Garamond

Library of Congress Cataloging-in-Publication Data

Names: Morgan, Courtney E., 1982- author.
Title: The seven autopsies of Nora Hanneman : stories / Courtney E. Morgan.
Description: Tuscaloosa : FC2, [2017]
Identifiers: LCCN 2016040433 (print) | LCCN 2016054462 (ebook) | ISBN
9781573660594 (pbk.) | ISBN 9781573668705 | ISBN 9781573668705 (E-book)
Subjects: LCSH: Women--Sexual behavior--Fiction.
Classification: LCC PS3613.O7425 S48 2017 (print) | LCC PS3613.O7425 (ebook)
| DDC 813/.6--dc23
LC record available at https://lccn.loc.gov/2016040433

Contents

For Mom and Dad

For Kian, always

The Seven Autopsies of Nora Hanneman

The Autopsy

Cause of Death

She stood in the doorway, arms stretched over her skull. The light behind her lit the right border of her shape. Her hip. The seam of her leg. A curving breast, the round, profiled head of the nipple. Thin hairs caught in the sun. The smooth limits of female pelt. She was smiling. Laughing. Glass breaking under water. The skin curled into goosebumps. The room cooled.

Manner of Death

Homicide.

Diagnoses

She touched him. They sat by a pond. They sat on a bench. They sat on the grass. Her hand touched his arm. The temperature beneath her fingers rose. A moment. The hairs on his arm straightened, caught in the warmth. She laughed. His throat loosened. His Adam's apple rose and fell. He laughed. Her hand was gone. His skin still warm.

Anatomic Findings

1. Cutaneous bruising and abrasions. Fingernail abrasions to neck muscles.
2. Extensive bruising to sterno-nuclei muscles below mandible.

3. Fracture of hyoid bone, thyroid cartilage, cricoid cartilage.

Opinion

She looked at the tablecloth. It was red. She drew her nail against the edge. It snagged. She rubbed the nail against her leg. She looked at him. Her eyelids fluttered. She looked at the tablecloth. She was smiling. She looked at him. He shuddered.

Circumstantial Findings

Nora Elle Hanneman was a 28-year-old white female. The body was found in a basement, clothing removed. External evidence of asphyxia, likely by throttling, noted at the scene.

General Description of Clothing & Personal Effects

Shirt: blue. linen. long sleeved. seven buttons. third button torn, missing.

Pants: denim. dark rinse. skinny. size six.

Socks: white/green stripe. calf-length.

Shoes: boots. brown leather. side-zipped. size eight.

Panties: black. cotton with lace edging.

Bra: black.

Jewelry: ring: silver. garnet stone, oval shaped. necklace: silver, onyx feather, received 28th birthday.

Signs of Death

Her fingertips pressed into his. Her neck arched back. Tendons stretched against the thinning husk. Lips brushed lips. Heartbeat rose against the rib cage. Pushed at its shell. Quickened. Her fingers twisted into the hair at his nape. Her fingers traced his spine, slipped beneath the loops of his belt. She lifted her shirt. She lifted his shirt. Breast brushing breast. Flesh against flesh. Breath in his ear. His skin lifted to meet hers. Hands curled around hips. His fingers dug into the meat of her. Hands tore down her spine. He lifted.

Circumstances of Death

The day was gray. The buildings gray in the rain. The road gray where he sat. There was rain. His forehead was wet. His skin. Nora wore a red coat. She stood in the rain. Her hand reached out. It wetted. She touched his hand. She touched his neck. His. Not mine, not me. She touched a man. Another man. His face drying beneath her fingers. The carapace I held her in cracking, her bones breaking open. She is becoming someone new. He grabbed her elbow in his hand. He pushed against the door. A glass door. They were inside. Heat began to dry their hair. She drying under his touch. I stood in the rain. I touched my forehead. Wet.

Identification of the Decedent

Ash-brown hair. Green eyes. Flecked with gold. Olive coloring, blue-tinted in the face. Green across the chest. ½ centimeter mole on left breast. It is her.

External Examination

Dark. The sheet white. The boundaries of her body. Distinct. Instantly greening in death. Instantly blurring. Composting, minutes after the absence of breath, into the white of the sheet. The entropy of decay catching the cells and tearing them away from one another. The edges of the expanding universe winning the battle against gravitational attraction. In one thousand days, a body turns to dust.

The body gray in the shadows. In the ambient light the eye captures in a dark room. The arm drawn up, elbow bent at the head. A breast taut below the exposed armpit. Lightly stubbled. Cells continuing to grow, to turn over and expire. Smooth expanse of stomach. Rising gently, softly at the navel, dropping into the rounded mound of hair. Knees, carved like chalk.

Artifacts

The following artifacts of putrefaction are present: Skin slippage, green discoloration of abdominal wall, malodorous gas, bloat of abdomen and other tissues, purging fluid from mouth and nose.

External Evidence of Injury

Her feet ran through the air. Her nails clawed. Biting into flesh. Drawing blood to the surface. Her eyelids swarmed, filled with white, closed, fell open. The irises green. Pupils clouded with cataract gray. Her torso lifted against the bed. Fell back. Lifted. Her body shook. Shook. Lay still. Again, she is mine. I kissed her. Again.

Internal Examination

Serous Cavities

The body is opened with a standard Y-shaped incision. The cranial cavity is opened with a coronal incision of the scalp. There is no blood or excess fluid in either pleural cavity. There is no excess fluid in the peritoneal cavity.

The epidermis molts and peels. Her insides are marbled and bulbous. White and pink slink together in pancetta folds, the wallpaper strips from her meat like from a butcher's hook.

I am three. The sun bloomed behind their heads. Light broke through their dark shapes and smacked my eyes. Floating above them balloons of red and blue and green, my small legs lifting from the ground. A hand, warm and thick around mine—inside my own melted like a feather. His mustache smiled at me and worm wriggled and I grew tall. From his shoulders, the heads below me bobbed like ducks, and I swam into the clouds.

Neck Organs

Significant hemorrhage is present in the dermis, fat and sterno-nuclei muscles of the anterior neck. There is hemorrhage in the intrinsic muscles of the larynx. Petechial hemorrhaging is present in the mucosa of the lips and the interior of the mouth. There is no obstruction of the airway. The hyoid bone, thyroid cartilage, cricoid cartilage are fractured.

The already flattened strings of a violin. Plucked by fingers into a damp song.

I am fourteen. I breathed and it tasted like mint. There were leaves all around and we sat beneath a tree. His hand slipped over mine and I licked my lips. My stomach beat, stretching into the shape of a wing but never tearing out. All the moments leading up to this one—his smell like lemon and gasoline, and the curl at the nape of his neck, and his half smile, and the way he looked at me like through a wall—rose up in beads on my skin and passed into the heat of the air and a fish swam up into my throat and he pressed his mouth to mine.

Heart

The heart weighs 272 grams. It is in anatomic position with respect to the chest cavity and vessels.

Hand-wrapped. Squeezed round, it fits. Squish. Squish. Saliva sticky, palm crevassed with lines.

I am twenty. The rain streaked or sat in drops on the window and gray was my favorite color. Gray is an opaque leech: it ingests orange or purple and bleeds it dry, never being not gray. Never claiming to be just gray either. I lay on the sheets, coiled beneath my back, just enough discomfort to remember that I was there and headlights against the rain flickered across my ceiling and my hands lay naked on my unclothed body and my sternum broke open and the room and the gray with a purple underbelly and the pale of the headlights climbed inside.

Vascular System

The aorta is normal and anatomical. There is no evidence of aneurysm, coarctation, or laceration of the aorta.

Snapping like rubber bands. Torn from flesh and wove like a super highway across the floor.

I am seven. Each strand pulled against my scalp and I closed my eyes. Her smell encased the air around me, not powder and lint, but her going-out smell, flowers and something rich as cheese. Her nails dragged against my skin and it coiled into bumps. She yanked the braid tight and called me pretty and kissed my head and then she was gone. Like dust particles in the window light she flickered around me and I looked at myself alone in the mirror.

Lungs

The lungs have a combined weight of 712 grams. The lungs are unremarkable.

She. Sliced thin. Stuck to the window. Salami-stained glass.

I am eighteen. I had already held her hand like bones sheathed in paper. I had already watched her breath slow to a tick and then exit her as someone quits a tent and I had already brushed the hair from her closed eyes and closed her gaping mouth. And there in the room was a vacuum and for a moment I was in it. My skin like her skin had become something disposable, not a shell but a wrapper, insubstantial.

Liver

The liver weighs 1,235 grams. The liver has a smooth, capsular surface. Autolysis of the liver is significant.

The most human part of her. Placed in my pocket. Still warm through the cotton.

I am eleven. My fingers crept beneath my skirt and my breath was bristly and hard to swallow—I lay back on my bed, air rubbing against the brink of me, still newly formed and fetal. My fingers brushing my edges. I breathed in heat and light and then the break of a sound through the room, the opening of a door. And my tummy rolled down, calcified.

Pancreas

The pancreas is anatomical in shape and size in relation to total body fat stores. On cut surface, it is lobular with interspersed fat. There is no focal calcification, fibrosis, or hemorrhage.

Jellyfish. Octopus. The day at the aquarium. Her eyes in underwater light. Swimming in beakers under fluorescent white.

I am nine. The parking lot was empty, wind blew at it as the light turned from sunset to the flatness of dusk. The doors to the school were locked. There was a little slack; they pulled to the click and then dropped back heavy into place. The halls, I knew, were as ghost-like and dark as the lot. The sky deepened, settled itself around my shoulders. Still, no one came.

Adrenals

Two adrenals are present. The adrenals have golden-brown cortices and white medullas.

Ancients ate adrenals for courage in battle. A boy went into the woods and killed a bear and absorbed his soul.

I am nineteen. It was a moment, a night, and cut against a black sky we were forever. Smoke filled our laughter and cut a track to space. Alcohol thickened our blood and it pumped slow as oil and warm through our chests. The air in the window slipped past too fast and the road of ribbon coiled out into the dark powdered hills.

Urinary Tract

The left kidney weighs 113 grams; the right kidney weighs 117 grams. The kidneys are symmetrical in shape and size and anatomical in location.

Tract. Tact. Intact. Tax. Taxis: Arrangement. Tassein: to arrange. Taxidermy. Derma: skin. Root der (Proto-Indo-European): to split, flay, peel. Temper and temple from the root word tempus—to stretch or pull thin. The body is a temple.

I am six. The river swirled black like monsters and frothed spit on their thousand lips. It smelled like fish, rotten leaves. The log reaching across; the giant's moss-covered finger, slippery beneath my boots. My fingers dug in, chunks of mealy bark splintering under my nails, time trapped in the sound of churning water. The air froze, time the iced surface. My boots crushed the frost-glassed grass. I fell.

Reproductive System

Examination of the pelvic region indicates that the victim was not pregnant at the time of death and had not given birth. There is indication of recent sexual activity but no evidence that the contact was forcible.

Uterus. Hustera. Hystera (Greek). Hysteria. Hysterikos (Greek): of the womb, suffering in the womb. Verduras (Lithuanian): intestines, sausage. Verdo (Slavonic): bucket, barrel. Woman is a bucket.

Vagina (Latin): sheath, scabbard, covering (for a sword). Root wag: to break, split, bite—split stick with a sword inserted. Woman is a split stick.

Vulva (Latin): womb, female sexual organ. Wrapper, from volvere: to turn, twist, roll, revolve.

Pudendum: external genitalia, especially of females. Pudendum (Latin): "thing to be ashamed of." Pudere: to make ashamed, to be ashamed. Root (s)peud (Proto-Indo-European): to punish, repulse.

Cunt. Root cu, koo (Proto-Indo-European): feminine, fecund.

Gestation is nine months. Gestation is two years. Gestation is twelve days. Autolysis—self-digestion begins minutes after death. In ten thousand days, a body turns to dust.

I am twenty-seven. My eyes were closed and against their dark insides his touch was color. His fingers tapped my stomach like piano keys. He played me into sound, and, when I opened my eyes, the sky was so loud I thought I couldn't bear it.

Central Nervous System

The brain weighs 1,175 grams. The dura, stripped from the calvarium and base of the skull, shows no epidural or subdural hemorrhage. The hyoid bone is fractured.

Cut into quarters, gaseous methane escapes in a green cloud. She rides the wave to heaven.

I am twenty-three. I left my apartment and twisted through alleys to where the city breaks open into a wide stretch of green and trees and the sun was yellow on it and it rained, a drizzle and maybe there was snow because how could it not have been everything, how could the whole of the spun globe not have been inside my body in that morning?

Gastrointestinal System

The esophagus is lined with white-pink mucosa and is intact. The stomach contains 70 milliliters of partially digested food.

Bacteria begin to eat the intestines, molecular death, putrefaction. The worms crawl in, the worms crawl out, the worms play pinochle on your snout.

Cadaver. Cadere (Latin): to fall, sink, settle down.

Torn with hands from the lattice holding it in place. Torn from the edges of the stretching spider's web. Torn like wriggling eating from the inside. This is where betrayal lives.

I am twenty-eight. There was a layer of glass over his eyes, like they sat five inches back in his skull, like there were boards nailed across and behind was dark and smelled like drying river grass, copper and the scales of fish. He looked past me. He walked past me. The place where he had sat in the cavity of my abdomen detached, unraveled from its scaffolding and pooled at the bottom of my pelvis. His hands reach for my throat. This is where betrayal swims.

Specimens for Toxicology

None.

Specimens for Chemical Analysts

None.

Specimens for Culture

None.

A Small Blue Heart [Shook Inside]

It smelled like spring, like wet bark and earthworms and the girls were digging.

"We can put the waterfall here," Anise said, bent at the waist and pointing across the emptiness of overturned earth, "and the roses over there, under the climbing tree."

"And daisies next to the pond," said Nora.

"Yes and daffodils."

"And lavender."

"Lavender stinks, Nora," Anise said, her gaze sharp on the dirt.

The girls dug their shovels into the chalky soil and it dusted their noses and made them sneeze while their mothers swept it from the kitchen and wiped what the wind had carried in from tabletops and piano benches. They hacked at rocks and threw shovelfuls onto nearby bunches of yucca and crabgrass. They worked mostly in silence, sometimes humming, sometimes making jokes about their balding teacher and sometimes Anise would hang, a chrysalis, upside down from the pine branch at the edge of their barren rock garden and watch Nora wipe the sweat of her palms against her jeans.

A ladybug landed on Nora's arm. She blew it off, she sang, "Ladybug, ladybug, fly fast away, your house is on fire and your children astray." The bug flew off without landing. Her kids would be okay.

The sun set early behind the mountains and shadows crossed the yard and stole the warmth from the air. Nora heard her mother calling from their house on the hill and looked up from her digging to where Anise sat in the crook of the climbing tree. She carried the shovels under the tree.

"Why are you looking up my skirt?" Anise asked, straddled over two branches. She laughed.

"I'm not," Nora said, flicking her gaze from the tree to the ground to her feet. "I'm waiting for you to climb down."

"Yeah right, lesbo," Anise said and her face was dark.

Nora turned and started up the hill, squinting her eyes at the night and trying not to wipe them.

"Wait, Nora," Anise called after her.

Nora brushed at her eyes with her sleeve and stopped, not turning around.

"Wait, Nora, look," Anise's breath rattled as she caught her. "A crown."

Nora turned and looked at Anise's hands, holding a woven ring of white clover flowers.

"It's for you," Anise said, lifting it, and Nora bent her head and let her put it on.

When Nora was a baby, there was a wind so strong blowing down the canyon it shook the tall house where she lay in a crib and her mother (like an old peasant woman) thought it was coming to scatter her like seeds. It didn't. Nora grew strong and silent and cased in a bubble of skin—just like us all.

There was still frost on the grass as they waited for the school bus in the mornings and the chill whirled around the legs they left bare, abiding the afternoon warmth. When the sun rose higher and the air was bluer, everything became crisp, like outlines sliced with a thin knife from a paper background—but in the mornings the light was milk, the hills around them covered with fuzz. Anise liked to hold hands until the yellow top of the bus peeked past the neighbors' house at the corner, and then she'd pull out a pack of gum and they'd pop their mouths like teenagers as they moved down the aisle.

Nora sat on her brick mailbox on days Anise wasn't at the bus stop and the neighbors' cat would sit with her, and they'd watch the birds on the telephone wire across the street. Sometimes it was sparrows on the line but mostly there were big black crows, purple in the rising morning. They'd start out in a chorus of ugly squawks, getting louder and more in unison and it sounded like an audience clapping, and then they'd drop suddenly into silence until a single bird would break the emptiness with three, lonely cries. And even in that quiet his call was unbeautiful. Oliver, the cat, would stretch on his haunches and sometimes test his claws at her ankles and she'd kick him to the driveway with a start.

Once, when Nora was stung by a wasp, Anise caught it against Nora's knee and held it by one wing in front of her face.

"Did you know when a queen dies, all the rest of the bees die? They just sit in the hive and rot," she said as she smashed its head between her finger and thumb, its stinger writhing in the air for purchase. Nora didn't tell her that the workers would make a new one, from a resting egg, dripping royal jelly into several larvae's mouths until a queen emerged. And when she woke, this virgin queen, she'd eat the others, still rolled in their larval gelatin.

They watched for the bus in the blurred morning and Anise rubbed her ring against Nora's palm and broke the silence.

"I'm going to dare Andrew to kiss you at recess today." Her grin was sharp but wavered at the edge.

"Anise, no." Nora pulled her hand away and rubbed it on her shorts.

"Yes. I am."

"Anise, seriously, please?"

"Oh come on, I know you think he's cute." Anise tickled her with sharp fingers.

"Ow, stop. No, please. Anise."

Anise stopped tickling and pierced her eyes at Nora. Then brightened.

"You don't have to worry, Nora, it's easy. Watch, we'll practice."

Anise moved directly in front of Nora, her legs spread, one on the outside of each of Nora's, their noses nearly touching, her breath like eggs and mint.

Nora didn't move.

She closed her eyes, blinked really, but the world went dark and the breath on her face was a wind and suddenly Anise's lips were against hers.

It wasn't much like the fruit she had practiced on while her mother cleaned the bathroom upstairs. And it wasn't tingly like when she'd found the magazine in her dad's dresser drawer, tucked between his undershirts. Anise's lips felt dry but tasted like the wax of her Lip Smackers and they were soft. They pressed and moved against hers with force, with life. Nora swung open her lids to see Anise, her tongue pushing against her own, her eyes held wide.

Anise stepped back and appraised Nora, a twitch in her nose. She threw back her long brown hair with a laugh but Nora saw how she peered from the corners of her skull like an injured animal.

"Alright, I won't tell Andrew to kiss you. You can kiss Robby Erikson. Just make sure he doesn't touch you with his warty thumb."

Anise laughed and Nora's stomach wrenched and folded as the bus rounded the corner.

As a child, Nora's dreams were thick and monstrous. There were slugs made of eyeballs and creatures with their flesh peeled away. She would wake crying and the pictures would project across her teddy bear sheets like stills from a movie, but one day they just went away.

They sat in the shade behind the pile of rocks high enough to block the view of the recess aide. Two boys lounged at the top of the biggest boulder, scraping off the dried green lichen, while three more leaned against other stones in the makeshift circle. Anise in the center drew hearts and stars in the sand with a narrow stick. Nora stood leaning on the outer edge of an empty rock, watching. She was glad to see Robby wasn't there, and she tried not to stare at Andrew, who kept his eyes on Anise.

"No way," Anise was saying, "Mr. Hurley's a perv."

The boys laughed and Andrew lobbed a pebble, which bounced off her leg.

"Hey," she said, standing up to give him a push off the rock. He fell to his feet, pretending to stumble and roll and she laughed.

"I'm so bored," Anise said, twisting her stick in front of her like a baton.

"We could play truth or dare," Andrew said. A round of nods from the other boys.

A breeze blew across the road and the overgrown yard, the yellow smell of dry grass. Anise scrutinized the stick in her hand, watching the knotty bark as it passed between her knuckles. She looked at Nora, and past her to the playground.

"Who wants to kiss you anyway?" Anise said, turning out of the circle and grabbing Nora as she swung her hair over her shoulder and they walked, hand in hand, to the swings.

The sky to Nora was cracked and she often felt her feet slip through and out to another side. Where the air was cold and blue. She would rock backward and touch the ground but she brought back in her fingertips the electricity of the air.

On the bus home, Anise braided Nora's hair and she watched the light honey-dip the trees and the ugly box houses and Nora felt that small hollow just below her throat fill with water.

"I'm glad you're spending the night," Anise whispered, the melancholy passing through the girl's hair and into her hands.

"Yeah," she replied, shaking loose her braid and the image of her mother, in bed before the blue light of the television. "What are we going to do?"

"Anything," Anise said. "We could watch a movie. Or make cookies."

"We could play dress up?" Nora said.

"Okay."

They lay on the basement floor in taffeta bridesmaid dresses and turquoise eye shadow. The news droned on the television upstairs while Anise's mom washed the dishes.

"Now what?" Anise asked.

"I don't know."

"Let's pretend our boyfriends took all of our money after the wedding and we have to become strippers so we can buy plane tickets home."

She threw the plastic tea set to the ground and hoisted herself onto the play table. The night was black—mountain black, the kind steeped in navy—and the recessed windows reflected Anise like a shadow mirror. The teal dress made her blue eyes bright and she pressed her hair and smiled unkindly at herself.

Nora rose slowly behind her, her stomach bubbled. She pulled herself up on the table. Anise started rocking her hips and tugging at her dress. Sometimes she'd bend low and pretend to touch or kiss invisible patrons. Nora began to imitate her. Watching her body in the window sway and roll, looking like a woman in the green dress with the padded cups.

Anise began to lower her dress now, slowly, past her shoulders and down to her waist, now to her feet. She kicked the dress from the table. Then her training bra. Finally her underwear. Nora slowly caught up. Her breath coming fast now, her heartbeat vespine. She couldn't look down at the imaginary admirers, she couldn't look at her own body stark in the glass, she couldn't look at Anise next to her warm and damp with sweat. She thought she might fall off the table, unable to fix her eye on something steady, when she caught Anise's reflection in the windows to her right. Anise's figure blocked hers, and she could look over her shoulder, her own head floating inches above as if her body had been zipped open and pulled down with the dress. Anise had her eyes closed and was moving to invisible music and Nora thought she was perfect.

They slept that night in sleeping bags on Anise's bed and when Nora woke, Anise was sitting in the window seat, looking out at the coming dawn.

"We should go to the creek today," she said when Nora was upright in bed and the birds were chirping outside.

The water was hazy pink and pine and the only sound, besides water over rock, was the girls' stitched breathing. They stacked rows of branches lengthwise across the narrow creek and padded the holes with rocks and slime gathered from the brook's floor. Water began to pool behind the dam, dissolving the sharp lines of the banks.

"You know," Anise said, "I saw you watching me last night." She had her back to Nora as she bent to add a stick to the pile at her feet and Nora felt air catch in her lungs. "I think you really are a slut," she continued, and she laughed, low and nail-like. "You're gonna be a slut too."

Anise looked back over her shoulder at Nora. She didn't have time to react. With a hand against each shoulder blade and the force of her charge behind her, Nora shoved Anise to the ground. Anise's feet caught on the dam and she fell face forward into the muddied water, legs up behind her.

Coughing, she sat up and slowly dragged herself to the grass, where she tucked her face into her knees and cried. Nora watched, her feet numbing in the water. The noise of broken breath over the gurgle of creek. She stepped to the bank and sat herself next to Anise, her shoulder melting into her wet and trembling one. They sat like that for a while, until Anise was still and Nora stood and reached for her hand. They walked together, Anise a step behind, back to Nora's house.

Nora was empty when she was born. Her mother bore into her mouth and blew respiration into her lungs, and like a balloon she inflated and then she was alive.

She almost stepped on it, and jumped back in a shriek. It lay on the mat at the door. One wing stretched out as if in flight, the feathers torn to reveal a stark tendon, the other wing sodden and matted against the bloody body. Part of its lower cavity was eaten away, but the bird was still breathing, and its eye darted in a circle. Nora spun and moved to the end of the porch, but Anise stood still a very long time and looked at the bird.

"Oliver," she said finally.

Then she lifted her foot over its head. Nora turned away but she heard the crunch of the tiny skull and it was cracking leaves.

They went inside and upstairs, past Nora's mother asleep under the covers, to the master bath. The light cut through the window at an angle, painted the walls warm. Nora turned on the tap and the brown Jacuzzi began to fill with water. The girls pulled off their socks. Nora lowered her shorts and looked at Anise. She lifted her shirt. They stood before each other and their eyes bounced across the other's parts. Toes. Shoulder. Knee. Navel. Breast. Then Anise stepped into the bathtub and looked at Nora, who climbed in behind her and they sat. Anise turned her back and Nora pressed the soap against it. The bar making wide circles, a glaze of white over the freckles. Reedy blond hairs dripping down from the nape of her neck. Anise spun her body in a circle, her bottom squeaking as it dragged across the tub. Nora held the soap, poised in the air before her, between them. Their eyes met. Nora moved the soap to Anise's throat, rubbed it over her shoulders, down her sharp collarbones. Rubbed it across her breasts, bubbles breaking over the goosebumped flesh.

She slid her hand down Anise's sternum and the skin pulled apart, split in two, rolled back to webby tissue underneath. The cartilage cracked loudly as the ribcage separated and beneath, a small blue heart shook inside. Anise leaned forward and their lips molded together, tangled around each other's mouths and melted into fired metal. Nora's fingers moved down Anise's arm and it flayed. Peeled aside in red and white flaps. Slicing away from graywhite bone. Cells ruptured. Vulvas rent open like buckets. Their bodies pressed together, coiled around each other, and she slipped inside. Layers of muscle braiding into one, bones clacking together. Their mouths gaped wide and Nora sucked and the air pulled from Anise's damp lungs into hers and she swallowed. Organs, like an offering, rose in Anise's mouth; a liver sat brown and shiny on her tongue. She passed it between Nora's teeth and she swallowed. Two ovaries, a uterus, pink and green, and Nora swallowed. Lungs. She swallowed. Blue heart.

The light was near gone when her mother came in to pee. Nora lay on her back, her knees bent against the wall of the tub, floating.

A Wing Unfolds in the Dark

There was silt on his feet and he slipped, but he was invincible and in a moment of sheer bravery and stupidity, the night wind at his back, stars salting his hair, he leapt from the roof, between the boughs of the sap-smelling pines and drifted, suspended, for a moment of sheer weightlessness—before dropping with a weighty snap onto crooked neck.

> I am the one who finds him in the morning.
> Who dusts him with blue jay feathers before
> going inside to Mother.

Grandfather had built the small house in the trees for him, of course, myself being too small and too girl for it, but the rope hanging from its branches was still my jaguar's tail that bore me to the sky with a tug.

Ever fascinated with flight, with the disruption and the triumph over gravity, he'd dropped me as a gosling toddler from a variety of windows, hitched to a variety of contrivances of fabric and wire and galvanized metal. I'd broken my tibia before he was made to stop by Grandfather and given, instead, access to the studio with its jar-lined shelves of nails and bolts and tempura paints, with stalks of veneer and flattened copper and pipes of all length and material, and he'd spent his days after school there, the dull lantern hissing above his dark and disheveled hair, Mother worrying after him for supper.

If I've forgotten what he looked like in those days, it may be because of the wolf mask.

There was a morning, dripping in spring, where he'd taken me, young enough still not to know better, to a meadow smashed tight beneath the noise of crickets, where thousands of the dull green things ratcheted skyward, hoping to never return to their dull green grass. He caught them, hundreds of them, in a burlap bag and carried the seething bundle several miles to the cliff above the rock quarry where we climbed and I slipped, again and again against the crumbling stone, to the top, which overlooked a small lake. One by one, over the fading of an afternoon sun, he lined each cricket at the edge, holding it between his index and thumb, each leaping without fail into the air and falling with a hiss to the water below. He had me hold several as they waited, eyes pointed to watch the others as they fell to their deaths, but they never learned. When all the crickets were gone and he shook out the sack, he turned to me. Now us, he said.

I clung to his shoe and hissed and he crouched on his hands and knees and with a swift kick tossed me back and propelled himself off the edge and into the white of the sky. I clawed tears from my blurred eyes as, lying on my belly, I looked into the opaque water below. When his head breeched the surface at last he was laughing and I closed my eyes and my mouth and didn't open it to speak for two weeks. He dragged me down the rocks when I refused to walk and he was whipped for the scratches on my legs when we reached home after dark.

In bed at night, a feather grows between each finger and each toe.

> I drag him heavy to the river, where he rustles,
> and I think tries to wake, but he lays there, his
> nose quiet, his mouth a twisted crescent and
> still.

Grandmother died before I was born, but she told me once, her hands on my mother's belly, do you see how the hip is shaped like a butterfly? If you tighten yourself, if you become narrow and sinewy, you lose the ability to talk with the bees.

She told me about her village, wobbling on the edge of a great cliff. She'd run to the precipice, breathless, and lift her skirt—and slowly and in crooked line descend on tissue-paper wings to the valley, stark and green below.

If you wonder how I remember, I'm sure I couldn't say.

At school, Susan Spiendel put glue in my hair and threw sand at me while everyone pointed and laughed. I'd sat behind the bricks and torn the grass into smaller and smaller pieces but it never'd disappeared. When we came back in for Spelling, Susan Spiendel sat and stuck, glued to her chair.

I kissed him that night before bed and when I lay down there was a small crunch. I lifted the pillow to find underneath a wet and sticky slidge, two eyes and rudimentary beak, the upturned edges of a tiny blue shell.

In the morning of that night—the one where he'd leapt to the roof of the treehouse, instead of climbing, fur-clad from the ground, where he tested the wind to see if she loved him—I watched him kiss the smallest Goldmund girl behind the raspberry brush at the edge of the world. She was dressed in blue, lighter than the sky, and her hair was plaited as a horse's down her back and her small pale nails scratched against her linty hem and she hummed through the passage of her nose. I had run, lost off the trail, tripping over roots coiled beneath leaves and I fell, tired and weak, under the ceiling of branches. When I reached home, Grandfather held me in his peppermint smell as I cried. He, that night when he returned from the brush, looked through me and went to sit in Grandfather's garage.

His voice was heavying and he became someone I did not know.

> I tie the branches together, with needles and
> wire and galvanized steel, and paint them blue
> as sky.

He went to see them, one frostbit morning, the steel birds turning their tricks in the sky. Father took him and not me, but I saw him standing there with his hands in his pockets, puffs of smoke from his parted lungs. A smile across his crooked lips. I watched their wings tear holes through the webwork, their propellers across the wind's back. He came home grinning and full of purpose. And spent many hours after in the dull glow of Grandfather's shop.

My sheath grew tight in the night, hardened into cuticle. I pressed against it, pushed my shoulders out, air blew through, and with a pop, I cracked.

I did it, I whispered in his ear under the tin dawn. I flew.

> The blue branches float on the water and spin
> in the current and the mourning birds begin
> their morning call. Trees stretch their arms and
> pinch the young sunlight into paper squares. I
> lay him sidesaddle across the raft.

There was whispering in the woods. I would walk for afternoons, sometimes with Grandfather, sometimes alone. The trail forked and to the left it looped to the river and then back to the broadside of the house. There was a pony that would follow me, eating clover from my back pocket. Sometimes there was a creature, with dark matted fur and a smell like the hollow inside of a fallen tree and I would hide behind rocks and trick him by covering myself in leaves. One day he caught the pony and sucked the blood from her body and the whine was like shivering in my bones. When Grandfather walked with me he would hold my hand and he would show me the plants and how they liked to be called and he would pick me leaves to nibble and he would smell of peppermint and smoke. There were places in the wood that belonged to me, not in the branches of the trees because I couldn't climb, but there was a burrow under a large stone and an eddy in the river where the water bugs mated and a tiny root-roofed house where two brother trees coiled their trunks into a braid and held hands.

In the winter the river would freeze over, then crack open from the force of water moving underneath. Chunks of ice caught circling eddies as steam rose. A felled log crossed it at its thinnest point and he would walk it like a tight rope, arms spread wide like a cross. I crawled behind him, my nails tearing into the flesh of the tree, my knees scraping the bark as the black water reached up to grab me. And then I was falling, the monsters below licking their eager lips—but a hand grabbed me, lifted me by my hood and dropped me, in the mud on the far bank.

> I wrap his wrists in twine, and around his neck.
> His elbows creak as they bend back.

He would sit for hours, for days, forever, in the nest of the house in the trees Grandfather built him and he would watch the birds, the clouds, the nothing as it filtered around him. Then he stopped. He spent time in Grandfather's shop and in town and in the raspberry brush. And I would lie on the flat boards in the rustling of leaves and listen.

> The saw is dulled but it cuts right through to dull bone and on my knees, using the length of my back, tooth-by-tooth I wear through it. Black blood drips sap-like at the laceration and his legs slip beneath the surface and float away.

The smell of Grandmother stayed around the house and the yard. It was calendula flowers and pepper and sometimes my eyes watered at the thought of it. Her hair was red and long and it kept growing in spirals. She married Grandfather when her countenance was young and white and they stood in the church and the trees grew over the eaves and brushed against the beams of the roof.

> His eyes need to be glossy bright, so I paint them with honey sap and stick river stones to their centers.

He lifted me onto his shoulders and I reached my hand sunward. It slipped between my fingertips and blackened between strips of white light. Higher, he commanded, higher. I stretched to my full length, my arm pulling against the shackles of its shoulder. Higher, higher. It blotted behind my palm and I grew warm. It fell away and he dropped me back to the cold grass.

> Where his legs had been, thin copper pipe secured with briny string. Leaves affixed to the

> bottom with paint, left to dry in the heightening sunlight. Wax-stuck feathers on the forearms.

The kite was painted red across the canvas and as it lifted it was perfect, the red in the white sky, and I knew it was Grandmother. Even though I knew she was in the ground. Even though when I dug my fingers into the soil I felt hers reach up and touch me. He said I was too small, that the kite would carry me away, that I'd shrink to an ant and then a speck and then poof! as if I'd never been at all. So he held me at my elbows and the string whipped from my hands and I remember the sound like the whirring of bees and the wind and the lift, like the grass reached down instead of up and everything stood in the sky.

I lay there on the forest floor, looking at the smoothness of his face, the blue of his eyelids. The world spun in upon itself, turned backward, and time stood still.

> Now you, I whisper. Fly. The raft spins in an eddy and the current carries it around the bend and I watch.

She pulls a string from each shoulder blade and out falls a wing, gray and shining.

The Watchers

Gregory's mother left when he was ten. I'm not sure how no one ever knew it. No one in the neighborhood. No one at school. But I did.

It's been almost two years now. I watch him every night with my Bushnell Natureview binoculars. Built for bird watching. Gregory is a bird. I watch him make his sandwich in the window. The curtains are eyelet and they are clean. There are no lights. He uses a camping lantern. He wipes up his crumbs when he is finished. He combs his hair and brushes his teeth in the upstairs bathroom. In the bedroom that used to be his mom's, he changes into pajamas. I close my eyes for the moment. Sometimes I peek.

When he turns out his lamp I turn on mine. I write down the time and a few notes about his day. I turn mine off too and go to bed.

At school he eats alone. I guess if he talked to anyone, they might know. He brushes his straight and brown hair from his eyes. Eats his apple in big bites. I sit alone too. Otherwise, they might know. I perch at the picnic table diagonal from his, an aspen in between; if he catches me looking, it's a small adjustment of my head to pretend to examine the tree.

Mom makes my sandwiches at night. Sometimes I come back later and wipe up the crumbs. Stick them to my fingers and lick them off. I am a bird.

"How was your day?" she asks. I sit at the table and look at her. Mostly I don't say anything. Sometimes I say, "Good." Either way, she smiles and nods. I wonder if she hears someone else answer when I don't. I wonder if there is a ghost that I can't hear that answers for me. Sometimes I think out of the corner of my eye I see one, sitting next to me. Today she is singing a song. My mother. Humming. It's sad, but she is smiling and I follow behind her and wipe up the crumbs and she looks through me and I wonder if I am the ghost.

The evenings after school are the worst. Before the sun sets and the lantern comes on. Sometimes I go across the street to the bushes. I pretend to be looking at flowers. Or digging in the dirt. But all I really see is a shape. I don't want to see his shape. I want to see the line of his hair. The shadow of his chin across his neck. I sleep at night in the windowsill. In the bay window my mom calls it. I call it a windowsill. I press tight against the glass and when it's cold my breath fogs a circle. And Gregory's house, it's like it sits on a cloud.

Today, the humming and the crumbs are too loud in my ears and I go outside. I swing in the tire. I cross the street. I dig in the roots below the dry tangle of rose bush. The thorns catch against my arms sometimes and I'm bleeding. I feel something and I look up. He is there, standing at the window looking down. I turn and run, my shirt tearing in the branches and I don't look back. I go up to my room but I can't go to the window. I stand back, against the door and it's dark in here and it's light outside and I know he can't see me. But I know he's still standing in the window. I scoot a few inches to the side so the bookshelf blocks the view. Even though he can't see. Can't possibly see in.

At school, I sit at my table but Gregory is not there. I see him come out of the cafeteria and walk towards me. I can't breathe and I close my eyes. Bury them in my arms. I open them only to look through the cracks in the wooden table and see my tennis-shoed feet below. When I lift my head, Gregory is seated at his usual spot. His back to me. I watch him eat his sandwich. Fold the plastic bag into squares. When the bell rings, he twists his neck quickly. He looks into my eyes.

At the end of the day, he is standing at the sidewalk where the schoolyard meets the street that leads to our houses. I loiter on the steps. He doesn't leave. Finally, I decide I will walk past him and home. I don't care what he thinks he's doing. When I'm about twenty feet away, he turns and starts walking in front of me. Down our street. Hands in his pockets. His neck tucked forward. I walk behind him and he keeps my pace, we're always twenty steps apart. When we get in front of my house, he splits left and crosses the street. I stop in front of my door and watch him in the window's reflection. He stops in front of his own, turns and looks at my house. Then he goes inside.

He turns on the lantern before it's quite dark. I'm in my room, back against the door, as far from the glass as I can be. I haven't moved. But I can still see out. I can still see the lantern light. And I move closer. Halfway across my room. I watch him eat crackers and cheese. I think. I can't breathe straight, can't get the binoculars from my dresser. I watch him play solitaire. I watch him change into pajamas. He is just a shape, an outline. I don't close my eyes. I watch him sit on his mother's bed and brush his teeth. He looks at his feet. The night darkens around the circle of lantern.

In the morning, he is standing at the end of our block. Leaning his back against a tree, facing my house. When I come out to the steps, he turns and begins to walk. I follow.

He is at my table at lunchtime. Sitting on it. His feet on the bench. Facing away from where I exit through the cafeteria door. I stand just outside. Frozen. The brown paper sack gripped in my fist. The turkey sandwich sweating in the plastic bag. When the bell rings, he turns and walks past me. I steal a glance at his face but he doesn't look at me at all. I go to my table, sit, and look out at the sports fields. On the wooden slat is a flower. White. Each petal torn and placed in a circle around the stem. Held with tape.

Tonight, when his house is dark, I run across the street, a box of matches tucked in the pocket of my nightshirt. I lay out the sticks on the steps, spell *hi*. I stay up all night at the window with my Bushnell's, but I must fall asleep before he leaves because I wake up, late for school, the sun bright, the steps through the binoculars empty.

I am kept after school for being tardy. Copying words from the dictionary. *Assiduous* is my favorite. It sounds like leaves on fire. Gregory's house is dark when I get home. My mother is humming and wiping with a sponge. The crumbs are gone. When she sits to watch TV, I throw the sponge in the trash. He doesn't turn on the lantern that night. The house remains black and I wonder what's wrong. I sit at the window, trying to see dark through dark through the binoculars, and I wonder if he's waiting for me to turn on my lamp. I don't. I fall asleep at the window, the moon creeping over my arms.

There is a brown lunch bag outside my door. I almost step on it. Inside are the matchsticks I left and some popsicle sticks, too. I wonder if he's returning them. If he's mad I left them. I stuff it into my backpack. I don't want to be late again today. He's not there at lunch, so I take out the sack. I push the sticks around with my hand and see a paper underneath, folded neatly into a square. I uncrease it on the table and it is directions. Step by step, a house built from matches and popsicle sticks. It has two levels and a front door. He's not there after school either. But that evening, before dark, the lantern comes on. I sit in the windowsill in the moonlight. Building a house.

There's no school today and I don't usually see Gregory on weekends. Except after dark. I tell my mom I want to make cookies and she smiles and nods and hums. I walk to the store, stealing glances to my right but I don't see any movement. I get butter and flour, chocolate chips. The bags pull at my arms by the time I get back home. I turn on all the lights in the kitchen and start mixing. My mother comes in and turns off the lights, the sunlight pouring in the windows, then leaves. The cookies rise in the oven; I press my face against the hot glass and watch. The smell of baking melts into the room and into my hair.

While the cookies cool, I go for a walk. I prefer to walk in the alleys. There are always strange things, strange smells in alleys. And nobody really notices you in an alley. You're invisible, almost. I walk them at night mostly. You can stand behind the fence and see in on the families eating dinner. Sometimes they're arguing. A woman with her head crying on the table. It's getting warm now and the families are in their backyards. A man in a hammock. A teenage boy mowing the lawn, his Walkman filling his ears, sweat on his shirtless back. A baby girl in one of those little plastic swimming pools. Her first time maybe. The mother laughing and splashing. The girl looking confused. I stand there for a long time, watching the girl. Her hands hit the water; it splashes in her eyes. She looks accusingly at her mother, the light wisping her hair from the side, then opens her mouth and cries. I laugh as she is swooped up and carried inside. On my way back, I pass through Gregory's alley and look at his house from behind. It looks odd. Everything looks saggy and worn down, the lawn is overgrown, one window is broken, a little playhouse turned on its side. Like when you think someone is young from the back, and he turns around and is old as snakes. Like Gregory is only keeping up appearances in the front. No lights are on and there's no movement I can see. I creep close to the fence. It's chain-link. I know I'm exposed if he looks out. I gently fumble the latch on the gate. It squeaks, that metal on metal screech that curdles your spine, and I run.

It's getting dark and the cookies are cool in the window. I stuff them into a lunch bag and wait by the front door. The glass is frosted; I can't really see out except the sunlight, which grows dimmer as I breathe. Then I see a change in the light. It's warm and yellow. Lantern. Time passes. The light disappears. I know it's moving upstairs. I run, fast as I can across the street. I leave the cookies on the front steps. I turn and run back. I make it as far as the walk leading from the street to his house. A door creaks open. "Hey!" I plan to keep running but that hey freezes me. My feet stick to the concrete. I don't turn around. "Come over," the voice says. "Tomorrow. Come to the back gate." My blood is so loud in my ears I'm not sure I can hear him. But I hear a click. The door. My legs can move again. I sprint across the road.

♦

The morning is gray and I lie in the window seat. It is rainy and I know I will never leave this spot. Gregory's house is dark. Curtains drawn. Even in the weather and I wonder how he can see or if he's sleeping. He's not sleeping. He's waiting for me. I know. I can't move. I French braid my hair. Bite off my nails. The curtains don't move. I get up. I put on my dirty Keds and stand behind the front door. I leave the door open, walk through the rain, around to the alley and to his back gate. I creak the latch open and stand there, rain wetting my hair, gathering it into clumps. He comes out of his back door. Motions to me. I cross through the puddles in the yard. I wipe my face, my eyes, under his awning and look up. His eyes are like turtles, green speckled with brown shells. I look down at my shoes.

"Want to come inside?"

The layout of his house is similar to mine, but it looks like it's under construction. Floor boards are torn away, some of the walls are only planks of wood, the wall part ripped off or broken. It's dark and the curtains are still drawn. He strikes a match behind me and a light encircles the kitchen.

"How do you get gas?" I ask him.

"I steal it," he replies, "from Gerkin's."

I look around the kitchen, peeling wallpaper, broken tiles. But everything clean.

"Come in here."

I follow him into the living room and in the center, a treehouse. Or a fort. I don't know what to call it. It has a door with a handle. A shuttered window that swings open. He pushes the door and we go inside. There is a small table, with two sandwiches laid out on plates, two glasses of milk, two chocolate chip cookies. There is a can, like a coffee can, a big one, and he lifts it and strikes another match to something underneath. He sets it back down and candlelight sifts through the punch holes and scatters on the wooden walls like stars.

"Did you build all this?"

"Yes. Do you want to eat your sandwich?"

I sit and we eat. Bologna and American cheese. I look up and he's looking at me. I find it hard to look at him close up. I wish I had my binoculars. But then he looks down, takes a bite of sandwich, and I see the way his nose bends slightly to the right, the dusting of freckles like powdered sugar. He looks up again and our eyes catch and we smile, quickly, look back into our milk.

"Do you want to take your clothes off?" he asks when we finish eating.

I look at the wood floor. Between some of the boards I see nubbed maroon carpeting, like the stuff in my mom's bathroom.

"No," I say.

"Okay." He stands up and takes my hand. "Want to look around?"

He leads me upstairs to his mom's old room. He holds onto my hand. The closet door is open, several dresses pushed to the side, and next to them hang Spider Man pajamas and a few T-shirts. A sleeping bag lies over the floral bedspread. A worm of sadness slithers through my chest. There is water in a bucket next to the sink. He leads me down the hall, the lantern glowing in front of us. There is a door, boarded up, and he reaches into the corner where a hammer lies against the wall. He lets go of my hand and starts pulling at the nails, taking the boards one by one. I take a step back and watch, his arms and back tightening under his shirt, small clouds of plaster falling from the wall. He sets the last board on the floor beside him.

"I haven't been back in here since."

He turns the handle.

There is dust everywhere. Covering the furniture, floating. Weird, because I read dust came from human skin. The walls look blue, but it's hard to say in the dark and murk. There are books open on the desk. Legos, Transformers. There's a stuffed pig on the bunk bed; it's wearing overalls. He pushes it aside. Lays down on top of the covers, curls up on his side, his back to me. I see his spine through his T-shirt, his ribs move up and down. Like a trilobite. I duck in beside him. Curl my arm over his stomach. We fall asleep.

I wake up to him pushing over me, climbing out of the bed. Pulling the covers out and the pig. I follow him downstairs to his small house. He slams open the door. Carries in the blankets. Comes out with a sledgehammer. Now he is slamming into walls. The ones dividing the kitchen and dining room. I step back and press my body tight to the front door, shielding my eyes from flying plaster. I close them. Listen to the pounding hammer. His breath, strained quick. It gets quiet again and I open them. He carries two-by-fours into the house. I hear him cutting.

"Can you get newspaper?" he asks without slowing the saw.

"From where?"

"I don't know, find some."

I go out to the alley. The rain has stopped, but the street is still soggy. I start walking down it. See some newspapers piled under an awning near the far end. There is a kid crying, a man yelling. I stop, put my eye to the fence. They are in their living room, silhouetted against the blue TV screen. The man has the kid's arm in his grip. He slinks away, but the man hits him across the face. The kid drops, to his knees, I assume. I see only the tip of his head through the window. The man's shoulders slump, rise and fall. I run to the newspapers, pick up as many as I can carry, run back to Gregory's house. He is standing by the back door. "It's ready," he says.

Inside his small house, the table is gone, the wood planks are stacked into a pyramid or a teepee. He takes the newspaper, starts balling it up and putting it under the boards with the covers from his bed. A pig ear poking out. He takes the matches from his pocket, takes one to a page, steps back. We stand in the doorway of his little wooden house and watch the flames grow. The wood starts to smolder, blacken, and smoke. He tears curtains from the windows and throws them inside. The fire eats them and gets taller, taller. We stand back against the wall of the living room and watch the house burn. The smoke blurs and stings my eyes. I cough. Not Gregory. He just stands there. Watches. It's hot on my face, it's not touching me but it's burning, like the sun, right up close. I think I hear laughing. I feel myself slinking to the floor, and then Gregory is lifting me. And then we're outside.

We cross the street to my house. The door is still open. We go up to the bay window. Cross-legged, we both fit. His hand lies next to mine. I feel the heat come off of it. I hear my mom's humming through the vents. He pulls a pen from his pocket. He takes my arm and traces the lines of my veins over my skin in black ink, fingers to elbow. When he's finished, he puts the tip of my thumb in his mouth.

We sit here, we pass the binoculars back and forth, you can see all the colors in the flames. The walls curl in on themselves, crack and fold like matchsticks, and we watch.

Monster

A fairytale. When you were born, your mother hung you from a tree. She draped a piece of muslin over a branch and swaddled you inside and rocked you for hours and months and years. When you were older, and you raised caterpillars in school, you understood that your mother had capsulated you in a cocoon, and you'd come out with rudimentary wings, viscous and unformed though they were.

A girlchild. Meet me at two, the boy says at your locker. In the parking lot behind school. Not in the parking lot, we'll go somewhere else, somewhere pretty, okay? The seats in his Bronco are cold, but the blankets make them soft. He is weighty and his breath smells a little like lemon, with a hint of vinegar and you like it. He rubs his hand under your shirt and pulls down at the bra. You rub your hands along his arms, the muscles sinewy but solid. Your breath smears the window. Your toes walk his shins. You arch your back. Your mind fills with the image of sheep. Of being at the farm as a child, leaning into their cage, of being thrown back by the electric fence, of the almost painful, not entirely unpleasant buzzing sensation that riddled your bones for the rest of the day. It deepens and warms as he puts his mouth on you. You skitter inside of yourself. You remember.

A monster. You stood. You waited. You watched. You saw her. Short, bobbed hair. Syrupy bangs hanging messy. Skinny legs poking from pink shorts. Shirt lifting to reveal a slip of belly. Her eyes. Lost on rows of plastic and pink. The familiar tug in your groin. You waited. Another familiar feeling. The panicked electricity seized your chest. Melted like metal. Milky hatred. You reached for your shorts. You paused. Looked at the ceiling. Fluorescents burnt your eyes. It was enough—almost enough. The cough rose up into your mouth. Copper on your tongue like you'd been running in the cold. And you knew it was not enough. You lowered your eyes. She was gone. You moved to the next aisle. Pink shorts. Bobbed hair.

A girlchild, dreaming. There is a robin pecking at the ants behind the bark of an orange tree near the window and the cat, behind glass, eyes it wearily. But you do not watch the bird, nor do you turn to watch your mother clucking through the kitchen behind you. Your eyes lock on a fuzzy circle of paint on the wall where a glass-framed family photograph once fell to the floor and broke. You stare at the spot without interest, with the resignation of the cat. Your pupils settle back into your skull and your daydreams are given more room to move about.

A monster child. You sat one morning on your mother's lap. The light dim. She trimmed your hair with sewing scissors. There was music. Coming through the window maybe. Or rumbling behind her throat. The furnace blew air warm against your legs. Your feet pressed against the concrete floor and were cold. You heard singing. In your mother's chest and in her heartbeat and in the rasp of branches against the window. You tucked your feet beneath your legs. Beneath your mama's skirt. And you were warm as hair scattered in clumps on the ground.

A girlchild lives in a shoebox panorama. There is a blue goose, long-necked and bent crooked against the walls of one of the bedrooms of the dollhouse, the one with the pink striped wallpaper. He wakes you sometimes in the night, honking sadly and banging his head against the paperboard ceiling.

A monster arrives, again. One summer, you worked in an ice cream truck. Watching the bare feet splatter against hot concrete. Watching small tongues lick dripping chocolate. From thin hairs on tacky arms. Watching their eyes glow at the sight of you. It was hot in the van. The gearshift sweat in your hand. The seat oozed under you. Gripped your thighs. There were the two girls in the street one day. Sledding on damp grass. Legs entangled on an orange saucer. They spilled out onto the concrete, their joined bodies skidding with a scraping sound. They lay, shaking with laughter. Mouths open, tongues hanging astride, eyes rolled back. They looked up and saw you. Naked like their laughter. Exposed in the open doorway. Possessing them. The girls screamed. Behind it was a sheer giggle. They scrambled against each other. Ran toward the house. You smiled. You drove away. The ice cream song playing. Trimmed lawns and spurting sprinklers.

A girlchild in the room. You lift the compact gently from your dressing table, like a silver shell, and slip it beneath your pillow although you are alone. You finger it gently in the dark beneath the covers and your heart beats loudly because you're holding your breath. You tug the chain on the bedside lamp and the light sighs across the white sheets. You open the glass and your eyes, green and lined with soft hair, surprise you. The mirror roves your skin, the shapes of you new but not entirely unfamiliar. The screen fills with your smile, your teeth, your tongue dragging across them; it fogs with the moisture of your exhale as you push your lips against it, dries at the batting of your lids. There is a creak on the stairs and you pinch the mirror shut, tug at the chain to darken the room and hide your head beneath the covers. The pulse pounds inside your ears, raps against your chest. Your mother peers in your door—shadow figure hovering, then closes it.

A monster learns a lesson. You put your hand on her leg. She struggled. She was easily overcome. She was easily held. In place. You lifted her skirt. You locked the hem between your teeth. You peered down at the beginning of beginning. You stopped, looked away. You had to hold yourself. In place. You would claw through thin tissue paper. Rip it away. You would ravish. You closed your eyes. Opened them. You were alone at the window. White sky filled every inch of the frame.

A girlchild sleeps. When you lie down at night, they fly in, the thick, furry-winged things and land on your eyes and lips and labia and drink while you fall into sleep.

A monster pulls back the curtain. One day you understood. That you huddled in dark corners because your malformed features couldn't stand the day. But that some not-small part of you yearned for yellow light.

A girlchild fishes at the surface of the still pond. Remember. The walls. The air around you was pink. And dolls reached out plastic arms and touched your hair softly and whispered *pretty.* You lay your hands on them, through cellophane windows, and they breathed you in. You arched your back. You smiled at your reflection. Spun your arms in circles. A shadow appeared at the end of the aisle. And you raised your eyes. A figure stood there. Brown hairs in crooked rails across his forehead. Hunched slightly forward, rasping out the mouth. You smiled, lightly, and moved to the next aisle. It was pink too. And it was full of babies. And you settled into their blue glass eyes. The shadow followed. You moved to the next aisle and the shadow followed. You looked at him. As if by mistake. You saw him. You looked away but you saw him. Poking from his yellowed shorts. A sad, gray turtle fallen from its shell. Your chest flooded with sticky. Like the day you walked from the store bouncing the orange ball your mom had not paid for. Like the feeling you had as you realized and you slipped it into your coat pocket before she strapped you in. How you hid it beneath the couch and never played with it. How your ribcage grew hot and tight when you saw it under there one day.

A monster cracks the bowl that holds it. There was the day that everything spilled out and you couldn't put it back in.

A girlchild, unthread. When you bled, the first time, the nurses at school were convinced you were pregnant, and they asked you, repeatedly, is it possible? And even though you told them, no, it's not possible, repeatedly, they kept asking, is it possible? Until you told them, no, it's not possible, I've never had sex, and anyway, I've never even had my period. And they looked knowingly at each other and clucked their tongues and gave you a pad. Curdled blood, blacker than red, birthing fibrous bundles of rolled yarn, thick paint streaked between your legs. And when you bled, that time, you swore that someone was inside you, stabbing you, slicing each organ from its connective tissue, ribboning your uterus in threads and pushing them slowly, down and out through your vagina. Just let me die, you told the nurses. And they laughed and sent you to the bathroom to change your panties, rusted and brown.

A monster before. Do you remember that moment: it was your whole life. It was a field. A sky, blue. Ready to burst its seams. Clouds, panting behind mountains. Raindrops breaking open on your nose. Everything contained in the bowl of that sky. Mountains reached up as the walls of your room. You lay on soft bed. The walls became the world all around.

A young girl watches a crack between worlds. And you remember the time the neighbor boy raced you to the woodpile and he won and he told you to pull down your pants because he won. And you stood there panting, watching a spider crawl in the cracks between the logs and you looked at the sun and it was bright and you didn't want to pull down your pants but he told you he won. And you remembered that you wore red tights under your sweatpants, that your mom helped you put on, that matched the red satin balloon on your shirt, and you pulled down your pants to show the red tights and you were happy because you'd tricked him. And then he told you to pull down the tights to your underwear and you had to because he had won and you smelled pine, and you crawled into a crack between the wood.

A monster (un)forms. You watched a spider one day, for hours; you watched her crack from her exuviae, watched her case split along the head and down the thorax, and slither out of herself, a callow. And you understood your own inchoate shape.

A girlchild slips back. There is the day that the boundaries blur. When the shape of your body no longer fits within the outline you had traced and you understand that it is no longer your own. That you are pressed underneath a paper doll and you can't find yourself in the mirror at all. You learn to put your smile as a sticker across your mouth. The corners turned up even when you are sad. You color over your eyes. Your pelt peels off in strips; you are flayed.

A monster wants. It was like that; it was like wanting to take yourself off. To belong to something else. To someone else. Wanting to be not all the accumulated layers of fur and dirt and hair—to just be air. To be hemmed in by somebody else was almost as good as never existing at all. No broken pieces, bone shards, scars. If someone would take you on, you'd loosen, your exoskeleton shattering into wings and unfold. If not, you'd take someone else.

A girlchild ravels. Your fingers rived one day, into forked tongues. Snakes grew from your hair, your toes; fat larvae wriggling against their casements. Scales erupted as your skin sloughed away. Apolysis. Apocalypse. Molting, too tight against your stretching skeleton, streamers of vellum dripping behind you as you crossed the room. The world bright and scratchy as you burst against it. Some new teneral. Some nymph.

An ever after. If you could be anything, it would be a branch in the maple tree in the yard, and you spend days practicing your art, reclining against the great boughs, slowly, breath by breath aligning the curvature of your vertebrae with the rivets of the bark until the wideness of boundary slips—lying still for hours watching only the sky. Cradled, by air, from the earth.

Motherless

When I was ten years old, my father told me a story of a man who swam the English Channel without coming up for a breath. He had been born with some amphibious defect, like webbed toes, except his was gills behind his ears. My dad told me that if I held my breath long enough, often enough, I could grow gills too—or my kids might be born with them. I spent two hours each day for the next three weeks in the bathtub until I fainted underwater and nearly drowned before he found me.

That was the summer Mom died and Dad spent every evening sitting in the rusted out Ford in the backyard, pulling weeds from between the floorboards and tearing vines back from the steering wheel. He said he was going to plant lilacs in the engine box, her favorite flowers, but he never did. When he was tired of picking burdock, we would settle into the cracking leather seats with cans of Pabst Blue Ribbon and he'd drive us to India or underneath the English Channel or to the dark side of the

Becoming motherless is an untethering process. You begin floating through space. Your home is sold and when you go there, to this new home that is now your dad's house, it is not comfortable like it is yours. It is not yours like it would be if she were there. You can still open the fridge without asking but all you will find inside is yogurt and mustard and a quart of milk. Maybe a carton of leftover sesame moon. Dad was a real fan of the imagination. He thought you could make anything happen if you just believed it enough.

That's why he was so pissed when Mom died. He was convinced she could have willed her way into remission. He would make her sit for hours on the back porch, that was in the spring, and he'd bundle her in the orange and brown blanket she'd crocheted in the seventies and he'd enact a play-by-play of her killer T cells attacking the cancer like Return of the Jedi. I'm pretty sure she always fell asleep, but it's one of the last times I remember her smiling.

By summer, he couldn't move her out to the porch anymore. Her arms were the same size as mine when I lay next to them, but white and flaky like bone and with skin hanging down like a bat cape.

It was the day that it became fall again, that you could feel a sudden crispness in the air, that you woke up thinking about apple cider even though you'd spent the day before in the sprinklers—it was that morning that Dad started packing boxes.

I can't stay in this house any longer, was his only reply.

It began in a very clean and organized way. He grouped books, photographs, knickknacks together and labeled each box with a permanent

chicken, but it will be old and maybe molding. There will be Wheat Thins and peanuts and black licorice in the otherwise empty cupboards. Instead of a room with your yearbooks and high school photos there will be a foldout air mattress that fits in the closet, that you can plug into the wall and inflate into a fairly comfortable bed you can sleep in with your son. There will be no toys for the boy. No extra diapers. You will maroon through your days, a ship set loose at sea, as if this forward motion were always normal, which it marker. As he moved from the living room to the den, then to my bedroom, and finally to his own, it took on a frenzy—landing in piles of clothes stacked atop cracked humidifiers, teddy bears stuffed into the crock pot with bottles of talcum powder, and jewelry twisted in a nest at the bottom of a laundry basket.

He began moving everything into the front yard. The orange metal lockers from the basement stood filled with moth-balled jackets next to boxes of ornaments, "Our First Christmas" inlaid in gold glitter; there were third grade curriculum books, Easter egg wrapping paper, silver-plated candle holders and antique flour sifters. Too much for him to look at, he said. Too much to smell.

It rained the next day on my horse books and my fragile collection, smearing the paint on my porcelain golden retriever named Misty. His old hi-fi from the garage sparked and snapped and Mrs. Basel next door told me, when she saw me loading my Barbies into an evac bus to escape the puddle flood forming in the cushion of the futon, to tell my dad that she'd call the police if the stuff wasn't gone in the morning.

Dad posted a sign in the night: Garage Sale. And with two changes of clothes, his tennis racket in a padded silver case, my violin and the picture of mom in her red scarf, we'd rolled Dad's manila (not mustard) Mercedes down the

is except the ocean
is wider, I mean, it
has no end, when
there is no port
with untied rope
somewhere, waiting.
It becomes difficult
to sustain a family,
to understand the
meaning of that
word, when you
are motherless. A
motherless mother
is an empty womb
leading back to
the beginning, the
alpha, the omega,
which is—mother.
Your son, or your
half of him at least,
was created within
your own mother's
womb and at one
point—was it nine
months or one
moment—you,
all three of you,
existed inside one
enclosed space, as
you existed in your
grandmother and as
a smaller particle, in
your grandmother's
mother as all
women do. After
existing together,

drive in the pink light of dawn. We stopped at the Grab 'N' Go for a box of doughnuts, an atlas, and a six-pack, and we didn't stop again until we hit state lines.

Southwest, he told me. In the dryness of the desert, wounds do not fester and weep, bread does not mold. We need dryness, girl. Aridity will air out the soul.

Dad gave me the map and pronounced me navigator. I sat cross-legged in the bucket seat and laid the wide book across my lap.

"It looks like Highway 50 will take us to the edge of Illinois." I flipped the pages on my legs to M27. "To . . . Missouri." I studied the squiggly lines before me. "To the Mississippi River?"

"That's right, the Grand Ol' Miss. And from there, onward west. Manifest Destiny!"

I squinted again at the snaking blue line.

"I've never seen the Mississippi," I said.

He wrenched to look at me. "Never?" he asked. "I thought on one of those summer road trips with your mom…"

"We mostly went up north, to the lakes, or east," I said, waiting for him to put his eyes back on the road. He was quiet.

"How old are you now, Nora?"

"Just turned eleven."

"Eleven years and never crossed the Mississippi. Never laid eyes on the muddy waters."

He was still shaking his head.

shackled in tendon and skin, it is a disorienting, backward sort of feeling to continue to exist when that solidity burns to ash. It is a topsy-turvy sensation to throw bits of ash and pebble into a windy February air and watch them settle into a name carved in a gravestone, not the name of Mother, but a baby's name, your nephew, stillborn, the grandchild that lived in her womb at your sister's conception, before you were born.

"Well, doll, we'll have to do this in style."

And at last he looked at the pavement spreading out before us.

I fell asleep and my dad shook me awake as we approached East St. Louis city limits. "She's coming up now. You can smell her."

We rolled down our windows but it smelled like Olney. After a rain. But dirtier and full of vehicles. It was beautiful and noises were everywhere. We spun through cars and trucks that seemed to come from every direction. We lurched right, then again, and then I felt gravel crumbling under the tires as he stopped on the shoulder.

Something in the air
becomes fuzzy in
the act of becoming
motherless.
Something in
the soil becomes
familiar.

"Out," he said, "get out." And he threw open his door in the wind of passing traffic.

I opened mine and saw that we sat at the edge of a steep wall of earth dropping down to a bank, and beyond that, a spreading sheet of water.

Mississippi—the word, the string of s's fluttered across my chest. It was wide and it was brown and it was laced across the surface with currents wrestling over each other in a mass confusion that looked also like a dance.

My father took my hand and he led me to the place where the shoulder fell away to only air over water below. We stood, leaning tight against the rail and traffic buzzed behind us.

"Let's walk it," he said.

I looked ahead. There was no sidewalk, just a thin concrete shoulder pressed tightly between the bridge rail and white line of the four-lane highway beside it. But he was already pushing me gently from behind, and I found myself shuffling forward. I couldn't look at the water. I wasn't even looking at the traffic really, not at my feet either. When we were back on shore, after I had dropped to my knees and clung in a ball shape to the bottom of my shoes, not yet half way across, I couldn't remember anything I'd seen, as if I hadn't been looking anywhere, except the saturated blue sky, hanging more like a weight than a color on my moist, sweaty skin.

I'm sorry, my dad said in my ear as we hunched together on the bridge and the cars passed. I'm sorry, I didn't know it would scare you so much.

I dreamt of her, most nights, but I didn't tell Dad. She was stuck, that was the problem. She kept trying to open the windows but she couldn't. The first time, the first dream, I said something to her, I can't remember what, about her being dead, something about why was she here. Or how. And when I did, she just stared at me, and then, without warning, started to cry. She cried hard and I laid myself over her and tried to wipe the tears away but my hands slid right through her face. I never said anything to her in the dreams after that. I just

You're forever
a vagabond; a
child without a
mother becomes
a nomad. It
becomes strange,
seeing families,
seeing mothers
intact. You
remember your
own mother,
certainly, though
not her smell
or her laugh—
those things
cling to the
sharp black cliffs
of your memory,
forever flitting
into darkness
when you reach
out to hold

followed her from room to room, trying to help her open the windows. She always started out young and healthy and solid looking but before I would wake I'd notice how thin and blue she'd become. We never got the windows open.

Sometimes I dreamt of a figure in my room. Standing in the corner mostly. More shadow than shape. It would reach his arm out to point toward me, and I couldn't move or I didn't want to but I felt a pressure on my belly and between my legs and I'd squeeze tight to keep something in, something that I felt like it was trying with raised arm to take.

their legs. But you remember her, and you remember her being Mom. But the spinning upside down sensation surfaces when you remember, because after a time it seems less strange that she is gone and more that she was ever there at all.

We followed I-70 as it snaked from M27 through J13 to F6 and outside my window everything turned from the dusty green end of summer Illinois to the yellowbrown of field after field of corn. At one point, somewhere between Missouri and Kansas and Colorado, somewhere between the Motel 6 with the indoor Putt-Putt course and the diner fried chicken and french fries with a Coke, Dad pulled the car to the side of the road and climbed onto the hood without a word. After a minute, I released my seat belt and came out and stood next to him.

"Climb up here," he said.

We sat on top of the car, my legs dangling against the windshield and looked out at nothing, all the way to the sky. We came from farm

Motherless becomes a nation.

country, but I had never seen flat like this. It was a swaying gold carpet, stretching out to the end of earth, straight out to the crack where it met Heaven. I don't know how long we sat there, but the sun was high overhead and it wasn't moving, and at last Dad hugged me to his chest and we got back into our seats.

The one place
you're sure
you know.
You become a
moonwalker.
The gravity that
kept you pinned
to the ground
is gone. The
umbilical cord
that connected
you, in cartilage
covered fascia,
severed.
You float.

Dad had asked me in St. Louis—when we were back in the car, my tears dry, my face still splotchy and purple—which way I wanted to go. I could choose anywhere, he said. I wanted to go to the Rocky Mountains, I said, because Mom had once told me about the leaves in the fall in the Rockies, I didn't say.

I didn't tell him, either, about Jackson Sawyer. Jackson Sawyer with the soft eyes and the breath that whispered, just a little in his nose as he sat behind me in Language Arts. Didn't tell him about the day I came up behind Jackson Sawyer in the row, the day I went to sharpen my pencil in the back of the class and how when I came back to my seat I saw, doodled in the corner of his notebook, Nora Elle Hanneman, and a tiny heart. And how when he'd seen me looking, he quickly flipped the page and turned red. And how he didn't talk to me after that, but I still heard the whistle of air from behind me sometimes and sometimes I would swallow deep and pretend.

The flat started to heave and lift. It stretched its back and carried us up. The ground exploded up in cliffs and pine trees around me and my dad drove. I thought sometimes that we might have skidded off, but Dad fixed his hands on the wheel and his eyes on the road and he drove.

"If you could go anywhere," he asked, "where would it be?"

I thought about it. I looked out at the clouds. "Mars," I said.

"Mars." He rotated his jaw. "That's a good choice," he said.

We went through a tunnel. The lights were eerie gray and it went on for miles. When we popped out, I looked back at the mass of rock cutting into the deep blue sky. The tunnel at the bottom, this tiny mouth spitting out cars.

"What about you?" I asked.

"Me what?"

You are always alone.

"Where would you go?"

He rubbed his thumbs against the steering wheel.

"Vietnam," he said at last.

He looked like my grandpa, before he had died.

We passed through an arch of yellowing leaves. At the top of the peaks surrounding us, snow clung in blue drifts, iced reflections of the sky.

"Mom said she would take me here," I said.

He didn't say anything.

"She sang me a song, at night, about her heart lying beneath the aspen trees," I said.

I thought then, for the first time, about her underground. About the coffin they threw dirt over. About the treeless corner of the cemetery. About her heart, as I lay my head on it, about the beat, becoming quieter like it was walking away, the spaces between steadily marching longer and longer.

I felt myself get smaller, curl into some part of myself, like my ribcage turned inside out and inside again, two sizes smaller. My lungs tightened and started taking on water. The sky was pinked and blurred. My eyes closed. I woke the next morning in a nest of pillows in an empty motel room.

I wandered the parking lot and peered through the glass into the lobby and restaurant. I didn't see him. I didn't see the car. I went back to the room and put on cartoons. I opened the blinds and watched out the window. The mountains had turned into high walls of sandcastle cliffs. Trees had fallen away while I slept and only pale green brush lined the highway.

I saw the Mercedes turn off into the parking lot and watched him unload two plastic bags of groceries.

"How you doin, kiddo?" he asked as he came through the door. "You hungry?"

We ate Fruit Loops in plastic cups from the bathroom while we watched Thundercats from the bed.

There comes a time when you understand she was always leaving you.

"Why are you doing that?" he asked.

"What?"

"Eating like that. Why are you eating one loop at a time?"

"I like to eat all the green ones first," I said. "They just added the green ones. It used to be just red, yellow, and orange."

"What do you do when all the green ones are gone?"

"I eat the yellow ones."

"Always the yellow ones next?"

"Yes."

"Why yellow?"

"It comes after green, in the rainbow I guess."

"So then orange?"

"Yes."

"And red."

"Yes."

"So then you have a bowlful of red loops. Do they taste the same?"

"The red?"

"Yeah."

"Yes, they taste the same."

"All the colors taste the same?"

"Yes."

"So why eat them one at a time?"

"It's fun I guess."

"Fun?"

I thought about it.

Like she knew from
your birth that you
were stunted with
crooked wings
and she'd have
to quickly teach
you how to fly.
She as one more
chitinized shell. Her
death just more
exuviae you'd molt
on your passage
to your own.

This is the moment
that you realize
that motherless is
not something you
became but a state
you were always in.
The condition of
your birth. Whether
she loved you or
didn't becomes
irrelevant. She was
never actually there.
You are defined
by absence.
Absence is a very
pervasive substance.
It can erase
memory. It can
chew through flesh.

"It makes me feel calm."

He looked at me for a long time.

"Mom used to save all of her red Skittles for last," he said. "She didn't even like the other flavors, but she'd eat them, just to save the red for last."

"I remember," I said.

He went outside and smoked a cigarette.

"Swim," he commanded. "Kick, kid."

Then the noise of him and the voices of other kids and the blowing air of the hotel poolroom thickened into the sound of water. Water covered my eyes, poured under my skin, as his shorts, tied tight around my waist, heavied and pulled me down to the grate. I swung my arms and legs and then I stopped. I sank to the bottom. I could see him leaning over the edge, make out his mouth moving. Everything gelled and slow. I felt my neck stretch apart. Felt the water slide behind my ears and pass into my chest, felt the blood pumping oxygen to my brain. The skin flapped open and closed, open and closed. I breathed.

"This is it," he said, "the Southwest."

He pointed out the windows at the red rocks breaking away from the dusty pale surface. Everything monochrome, striated shades of red. Sprinkled with sagebrush.

It was beautiful. It was quiet and very very lonely.

Plateaus and canyons and hills of red rock rose up through the windshield and my dad drove toward the Grand Canyon. It was something he'd never seen and I think we were both nervous. We sat quietly through most of Utah. When we passed the sign welcoming us to Arizona, he began to talk.

You carry around a small hollow place, a little porcelain vase painted with birds—and no one can reach inside it, not even your son. But he can run around it, he can rub his back against it, and when you put your hand on the ceramic, it feels warm to the touch.

"Did I ever tell you about Mexico?" he asked. I told him that he hadn't.

"It was just after I left the army. Me and Nate Matthison took our pensions and bought a VW bus and drove it across the border. We spent four months, just putzing around that country, and believe me, you've never seen anything like it. Oceans and cities and ruins, forests that make these ones seem dim. We'd go to the universities and follow the kids around. Ate where they ate, drank where they drank. It was the freest I've ever been in my life."

Desert passed.

"But your mom called, sent me a telegraph actually, said she was calling off the engagement. I took the next bus to Mexico City and flew to Chicago. Nate stayed on, kept heading south. Settled in Guatemala eventually. Think he owns a coffee plantation or something there."

The sandy hills were swallowed suddenly by a large pine forest, strangling up in thin patches at first, then ripping away the sky in my window.

"Do you ever wish you'd stayed?" I said.

A lake broke in slivers between the green.

"No," he said.

We sat in the car for at least ten minutes in the parking lot of the visitor's center. We didn't say anything, just looked out the windshield ahead to where the ground seemed to fall away. We couldn't really see the cliff end, we weren't at an angle to see in, but we could tell the point where the earth was suddenly gone. Finally, he got out. He came around and opened my door.

He kept his arm around my shoulder as we walked to the edge. As we approached, I could see the other side and I could hear a wind blowing between the two. Lost, like it fell off and couldn't find its way back.

They got Skype in Heaven.

For the first few years or so the lines were blocked, as you can imagine, because millions of people have loved ones to contact in Heaven. But I tried, every day I would sit listening to the droning ring with its otherworldly quality, which I think it took on only because I was calling Heaven, since, after all, it was the same ring I heard when I called my aunt in Chepeekwa or Miss Deeter down the street who could never figure out a cell phone but had somehow mastered Skype when the landlines were dismantled. I walked Miss Deeter's dog. But at last, after years of calling, the video-loading icon started spinning its doughnut circles and I scooted up my chair and stared into the screen and suddenly there she was. I don't know if the video system works differently in Heaven, but when my dad asked what she had looked like, old or young, sick or well, I had a really hard time explaining. She was all of them. It was like the video was on a really slow time lapse (or maybe really fast) and I watched her change from a young mother at my birthday parties, to a bag of loose skin dangling over tiny chalky bones (which couldn't have been more than forty-nine since that's as far as she made it), back to almost a child. I even saw her mouth, wide and gasping like it was, like it always was in its funny way when she slept once she started chemo—though it was not so funny because she was sick, and it was not so funny when she was dying, and it was not so funny as she lay in her casket with puffy chipmunk cheeks and you knew they must've had to crack it shut. So I saw it hanging open like it was in its funny/not so funny way, with the row of small bottom teeth standing guard before the bottomless chasm. I saw her mouth gaped open like it was as I tried to peer into the infinite that was trying to escape in strangled breaths. Until it did. Until the last short shot of air whimpered out and all that was left was a carcass. And as I sat on her bird bones on the tiny cot, still staring into the cavern that once led to her, I shook my head violently back and forth because it's a very difficult thing for a mind to wrap itself around—a mother becoming a corpse, just like that. Now it seems to me that it may sound very creepy and grotesque, this shiny, somewhat see-through video projection of my mother, morphing from child to chemo-victim to gaping hole while she asked me about school and my father, but I think it's just that it's difficult to describe. And also, she was very pixelated. I asked her to tell me about Heaven and she said the weather was cold that day but she had a warm sweater. Why didn't you ask her if they had seasons, my dad later asked, but I hadn't thought of it at the time. She blew me a kiss and I told her I'd call tomorrow, but I didn't.

The Birdgirls

I have a little bird. I keep it in a box. I tied a red thread around its foot. I open the lid and it chirps at me. Its head cocks to the side, to the other side. Its neck bones move outside of time, like a tape started and stopped, like you blink between one position and the next. Its eyes are black beads of water going back endlessly. I see my face in them. I see pterodactyls. Its eyes never blink. Its head cocks and turns on the stop clock of time. I have a little bird in a box and I put some twine and feathers in the box and it made a nest. I took out the nest and put a mirror in the box so the bird could see itself and think it was not alone. I let the bird fly and I hold the red ribbon in my hand. It flies out and the thread grows taut and it tugs against the leash. It flies the other direction until the thread reaches its length again and I tug it back, the bird, and then it starts to fly in circles and

Do you remember the treehouse we played in when we were kids? The one grandpa built? With the window that latched and the wooden ladder stairs and the curtains. Do you remember the carpet and how the bark would fall off the pine trees and stick in the knolls of the rug until it was so scratchy and rough and sappy like the trunk of a tree itself? Do you remember when you hid frosting in the little lockbox we kept in there, frosting in a can, and you would sneak outside and eat it with a spoon because Mom was never looking but do you remember how you left it out once and the squirrels chewed the plastic lid and made little squirrel bite marks it spins around and around over my head. And I laugh. I have a bird in a little box and it's starting to shed its feathers. It's making a nest from the feathers. The nest is nice. Its feathers are falling out or its plucking them with its beak when the lid is closed and great wide patches of bird skin are starting to show. The remaining feathers droop from its wings and I see, without the others to hide it, where each brown feather pierces a little hole and I see the bare pimples around it, bumped as if it is cold. Little white hairs cluster like soft whiskers in the barrenness. I pull a feather and the bird shakes. Vibrates. But makes no noise. I pull another. Its featherless wings open and fold. I close the lid on the box. I pull out each feather, one by one, and I put them in my mouth. I stick them to my arms amongst the light hairs. They dry on my arms and some I swallow and now the bird is almost bald, all pink callow skin except the tips of its wings and the hairfeathers on its head. My bird shivers. Its nails scratch the mirror on the bottom of the box as it scrambles and shakes its wings. The red thread around its foot is loose. The thread is blood and it drips on the box floor. The thread has fallen and sits in a loop at the bottom of the box, a thin red nest.

in the frosting? Remember the little pink imprints of their tiny mouths?

Did I ever tell you that that's where Ritchie Hogan went down on me for the first time, in that treehouse? Before I even knew what that was. Like licking pink frosting from the spoon, because Mom was never watching, and my mind swirled like his tongue, before I even knew what it was. I wrote his name, RH + NH, all over my binders. I wouldn't even have to give up my letter. Before I even knew what it was.

The rain is beating against the window, and I'm supposed to be working, but all I can remember is this.

I go outside and light a cigarette. That's not true, I don't even smoke. I just wish I did. Especially on the days like this, the gray ones. I would start. But the smell. I hate that smell. Also, someone once told me that people smoke because they want to die equally as much as they want to live. And that made me want to start, and stop, equally.

At least let's sit on the stoop and look at the rain. And wonder why it's so much more satisfying than the sun. And wonder why it matches the wallpaper of my soul. And why I've always preferred the brown night sky and black trees to just about anything else there is. Even the treehouse. Even the swirling sensation of somebody's tongue. Even cigarettes, even real ones.

There's a picture of us when we're little. A family photo. In front of the big blue van with the silver stripe and the fake leather seats that Mom drove us in every summer to Illinois. The week before the trip, we'd cut holes in old rainbow sheets, remember, for the seat belts to go through, because the seats got so sticky and hot and we'd lay across our own row and play car bingo or just sit and sweat and watch the cornfields pass by. But the photo is not on one of those trips. The picture is of us, all of us, camping. And we're all in seventies' puffy vests and I have a bonnet on my head, which is weird. But the sky behind us is thunderstorm sky. It's aluminum and luminous and the light it paints us in is electric and unspeakably beautiful. I don't remember the night. Don't remember if it stormed and we went home. It must have. That sky. But I remember that I was never afraid of the woods.

I had an imaginary friend. It didn't have a name because I was actually pretending to have an imaginary friend. I mean I really wanted one, but I couldn't make myself see one. I didn't really *believe*. Probably there were several, with several names, because they weren't real so they came and went, changed names, on my whim. Probably you told me I had one, so I did. Probably you changed their names when you felt like it. Do you remember how mad Mom would get? How out of control the world felt because you never saw it coming. Everything would be fine and suddenly she'd break and the whole earth would tremble, like it was glass about to crack, like it was thunder shattering the ground. I heard a story of a woman who lived in a high apartment building with large plate windows and was once watching a storm, her hands pressed against the glass, lightning and wind and all of it. Suddenly, the wind blew hard and the glass shattered, crumpling against her in tiny, knife-sharp shards. I don't remember if it killed her. But it was like that, wasn't it? I would fight with her; you never did, you would take your frosting quietly to the treehouse. But I would. One day, my imaginary friend started a fire and burnt the treehouse down.

In seventh-grade gym class, in those hideous blue uniforms, with the stripe of tape across the front where you wrote your name, the ones that smelled so bad, like gym, like dirty metal, no matter how many times you washed them, we had a unit on gymnastics. They had a full setup, balance beams, uneven bars, rings, the whole deal. Bryson Freck, who had been my boyfriend the year before, bet me that I couldn't do a flip off the bars. I remember the air buzzing past my face; I remember my feet hitting the ground solid. And he told me, after I'd proved him wrong, that I was ugly. And in ninth grade, we fucked in the back of his car and he called me pretty and breathed into my neck but that first word was buried inside the other word, all the other words. Something in me shrank. After, I smoked a cigarette.

It was like being unzipped, you remember. The thing of it, the painful part, was knowing that it was happening. Like a surgical patient that's been anesthetized, but that nightmare where something goes wrong, where they're drugged to the point that they can't move or speak, but not to the point that they're unconscious. Not to the point where they can't feel pain. So you watch and feel it happen. You don't understand it exactly, you don't know why or how, but still you know, that something, some solid and pulsing thing is being cut out, ripped even, tendons tearing and snapping like rubber bands.

The things we remember are strange. I remember this gold coat I used to have. It was shiny but it was a sport coat, not a sports coat, but like a sports team coat, with red elastic lining at the edges and a team decal on the breast. I think it was the 49ers, that's why it was gold. I pretended I was a ball player. I was a tomboy. But a princess ballplayer, I was that kind of tomboy, and I wore the jacket everywhere with dresses and cleats. I loved it and I remember playing soccer on the driveway in it, back when the driveway was still gravel, not paved, and it was cold so I put my hands in the satiny pockets of that jacket. Mom told me to put gloves on, that I would fall, but I didn't. Didn't put gloves on. But I did fall. I tripped and landed mouth first in the gravel and busted my lip. I bled. I told you so, she said.

I didn't fuck Bryson Freck in the ninth grade. I didn't have sex until I was twenty. Because I wasn't in love with Bryson Freck. I was never in love. And I wanted to wait. I wanted it to matter. Except I didn't wait for love, or even mattering. I got tired of that, I got tired of waiting. So I slept, one night, one morning actually, with some random guy who didn't mean anything and whom I meant nothing to. I had a friend at that time, a good friend, who loved me. I could have slept with him if I just wanted to. But after all that waiting, I didn't want to be loved. I wanted it to be nothing, I wanted it to burn. After, I smoked a cigarette. Really. And that's when that thing, that live, bleeding thing that had been torn out of me I thought, somewhere around thirteen, that thing that was far away I didn't know where, started to ache. Do you have one too?

I peeled my clothes off in the blue light from the window. He was in my roommate's bed. My roommate was out of town. I stripped and stood there, then climbed into my own bed. We talked, from our beds across the room. The sun started coming up. Strips of light on my pillow now. He came over, got under my covers.

This feels trite. Self-indulgent. Someone said that, once. It seems so naked. Unimportant.

You lost your virginity at fifteen. Later, you told me it was rape. It was date rape. At prom. So cliché. The terror of cliché. Why do you call it your first time?

Actually, I had sex when I was fourteen. To beat you. In the basement but I pretended it was in the treehouse where Ritchie Hogan swirled the sky. When I was little, I knew my body and the places it brushed against the air and the places it connected to the ground. It was solid and the pulsing blood wrapped tightly under lamina. Now how to explain this, but you should know it too. It wasn't that we were opened and something was stolen. It's that the sense of ourselves moved from inside that tight membrane to somewhere outside. Somewhere else. I didn't know where I was.

My cunt began to groan, grew scales and teeth.

Did I ever tell you about the time I walked in on Dad watching porn? I can see him now, in the blue light, hand pulling quickly out of his shorts. There was something so sad and vulnerable about it. He changed the channel and I asked him whatever I had come to ask him. I told him good night. Went to my room. I felt inside out.

Actually, I had sex with a monster in the basement. With four dicks and swirling snake hair. When I saw myself, I froze.

But the sex isn't really the interesting part. What I mean is, that's an oversimplification.

I was a tree climber when I was a girl. You weren't. You just liked to go in the treehouse for your frosting. But me, I loved the trees. There was something to it. The sense of being both in the sky and tethered to the ground. Also, the sounds are different up there, amplified almost, like a hard shell bounces everything back at you. But also, and here's the part I don't want to say, it was like being held. When Grandpa died I went into the treehouse, for a long time I sat there and just looked out, and I don't know what I saw but I have a memory still, of being there, shadowed, looking out the window at bright light. When Mom died, the treehouse was gone and anyway, we were too old for it then. And anyway, that sense of being held, of being a body touched by ground and air, was long gone by then.

My body became a nest of feathers—a human head popped out. The squirrels looked at me and chattered. I opened my mouth and song came out. Boys fell to the base of the tree, and I ate them.

What is the first time? Ritchie Hogan spun the sky. Sam Brownwell pulled down my pants behind the woodpile in second grade and pressed his hand against me. I found the tape my dad was watching when no one was home. Two girls, their pale white breasts full and round, heaving. They were prostitutes in an olden-time brothel. One was nervous, waiting, the second was initiating her, preparing her for the men who watched through a crack in the door. She slid her hand slowly down the other's stomach. I felt what I didn't feel with Ritchie. What I didn't feel with Bryson Freck or any of the boys in the basement or the guy in the morning in my roommate's bed.

Actually, it was kind of comforting, this is what you're going to feel, see, it's beautiful?

A Zillion Scattered Lines

See the car flung to the side of the road, one tire hanging off the gravel over the ditch. Purple gleam in the headlights. Like they'd been hit, like they'd been shoved to the shoulder by a bulldozer. See that tire, the front passenger side, that had blown.

The crystal is wearing off and the lines are starting to blur and I'm drifting. And I keep seeing her, there in front of me, in the road. She's so real I could swerve except I know it's not her and I know she is home in Missouri with a bed and a man and that in any case, she never would be wearing that nightie in the road.

See the girls waving their arms on the shoulder. One foot strewn astride, hip lightly cocked. Hair thrown in the wind. See laughter in the air. The radio still playing. The who gives a fuck.

My custom suspension seat bounces as I hit a bump. My custom blue leather. The CB cracks. Night spills in the window and the crackling voices the only thing holding out the dark. Kansas City by morning. Atlanta by Tuesday. Nothing but corn. An ocean of sameness. But what your mind does when everything is flat, everything is same. The digging thoughts that burrow through. Little insects, chewing through the surface of what you remember and what you never did. Hungry little worms, nipping their tails, biting their nails, scratching the gray matter for more crystal, more crystal. I pull out the bag. Knee under the wheel, I pour a line across the back of my hand.

See the girls walking out into the fields. Lighting a joint. See the small orange dot in the huge of the black expanse. See infinity.

The worms grow wings. Thoughts again like moths. Flit. Flit. I roll down the windows. The air is cold. The air rolls like marbles across my face. I remember her in bed. The shape of her body rolls like marbles across my mind. The curve of her breasts, the roll of her hip into that valley down and down. Warm and moist. My hand sliding down. My hand on myself. The thoughts jump, flit. Slow down. The man in her bed now. I push him away. Slide my fist into the soft flesh below the cheekbone. Hear it creak. Slow down. I push the brakes. Something flashes in the high beams. Purple gleam in the purple night.

See the girls as they return to the roadside. Laughter pouring out like smoke, like snakes. Dancing now. Shaking. Waving their arms. Brake lights in the flat night. Gone again. See the shoulder now. The gravel spitting out under monstrous tires. Headlights break the glass front of sky. See now the semi pulled to the edge. Huge in the hugeness. The girls look at each other. The girls laugh. A man lowers from the cab. His boots crunch.

This time she's real. But it's not her, it's girls. Two girls on the side of the road, their Civic nearly in the ditch. Nice little seat covers too. Shaking and flipping their hair against the nothingness night. Waving and flagging and anyone could pull over. Anyone could reach them. Any moment and they could be gone. I drift the rig to the shoulder and my heart is beating fast and my thoughts insects circling a lamppost.

Here the car, here the semi lined up on the white line. Here three bodies, circling the car like moths. Hear the girls' laughter. Their questions.

Their tire is blown clear out. *Do you have a spare,* I ask them. They wrestle around each other, bodies bumping, arms entwining and untwining as they move to the trunk, they giggle toward each other. I take the spare, the jack, move to the truck for more tools I don't need; my chest puffs in the cold air, the muscles of my arms expand and press against my shirt. I watch them as I change the tire. Watch their legs. How long since I've seen girls' legs, not through the glass, not immobile against the seat from above, but moving, alive, pressing tight against the fabric of their jeans as they bend and step. The crystal is still fresh and my blood presses tight against the capsules of my veins and my ribs warm and heave. I take my time. I watch their legs. I look up at them and smile, they smile. I want them here with me. I take my time. *Five hours to Kansas City going seventy-five,* I tell them, *on the spare, at forty-five max, you'll get there by tomorrow afternoon. There's a Walmart just outside of town, they'll get you set up,* I say. *No, no,* they cry. *That's too late, we'll miss our friends, we have to get there by morning, we have to be in New Orleans by tomorrow night.* They say, *What's your name?* They say, *Thanks for your help.* They say, *What else can we do?* Their wide eyes open and shut. The night pours in and out. Deer in headlights. Coyotes on the hunt. The worms whisper in my ear.

See the man pacing the car. Measuring his steps. Tucking his denim shirt deeper into his jeans. Shakes his belt. He returns to the truck, circles, returns to the car, circles. See the girls split, one circles the car clockwise, one counterclockwise. The first meets the man. She smiles. She laughs. The second comes up behind. He turns. She smiles. Laughs.

I want to keep them with me.

See now, the man lifting the gate on the trailer. Hear the rattle, the scrape of metal against the night. The girls sitting on the trunk of their car, leaning almost imperceptibly to the right, except the one girl, the one with dark hair, her neck follows the force of gravity and she lowers her head against the other's shoulder. Their hands are looped around each other's.

I look at them, at the car, at my truck. Back to the car. Back to my truck. Weighing the words. My options. I want their laughing and their voices and their legs. They turn around and I look at their asses, jeans tight, pulling up around their cheeks. I don't want to. To drive down that long white line and leave them back in this night and be alone with the crackling and with her, her body in my mind. Their laughs ring my ears and they warm against the cold air. I look at them, at the car, at my truck. *This car could fit in my trailer*, I say. They look at me, look at the truck, look at each other. They laugh and laugh.

See the metal ramp lowering. See headlights on in the dark. Cars passing. Seeing. The man gets in the car, the music stabs at him and he reaches to turn it down. Ruffles his graying hair. He drives the car forward. See the car swallowed into the trailer.

The girls stand behind and watch. They look at each other. Their bodies shrug.

The light-haired one says, *My name is Nora*, she is Nora now. The brunette says, *My name is Kira. C-e-i-r-e.* Now she is Ceire. *Gary*, they say, *Gary, are you married*, they say. They climb into my passenger seat together, side by side, legs winding. They bounce on the hydraulics and laugh. *Where are you from, Gary?* Missouri. *What's your wife like, Gary?* Marie. Gone. *Where you coming from?* California. Three days now. One night of sleep. I guide the truck out into the nightsea and marvel at how unalone I feel. How solid their bodies in the cab, their voices spin round and fill everything. They're on their way to New Orleans, Ceire's got a boyfriend playing in the city. Time passes and they grow quiet. I want their noise. I want the sound of them. Their eyes swallow up the night.

See the faces against the blackened windshield. See the three bodies, cased in metal and glass. See the man glancing his eyes to the right. See his hand scratching the knee of his jeans. See the girls on the seat. Their legs pressed against each other. Their hands rubbing gently the knee of the other.

Ceire yawns. *I need coffee*, she says. I hesitate, but the insects warble in my brain. *Want a bump?* I ask. Their eyes slowly roll to each other. Their faces dark. It's quiet and I open my mouth to inhale back the words, balloons tied with strings from my tongue. But they laugh. They laugh and laugh. *Whataya got, Gary? Whataya got?*

Hear the buzzing now. Insects. The sounds consume the world. The voices running fast. See the stories winding like thread in the air. Weaving around ankles. Their wrists.

Since seventh grade, they say. *She moved to my town from the West Coast,* says Nora. *There was this girl, this mean girl, this bully, and the first day of school Ceire just decked her. She hit her, right in the eye. We were best friends after that. She was my first kiss,* Ceire says. I chuckle. *Tell me,* I say. *Tell me about that. I was there when she lost her virginity too. Well, not there,* Ceire says, *but she left the light on. So I could see.*

See Ceire standing, her dark hair in the dark, shadows all about her face, her eyes piercing into space, the glow of a lamp from inside the window warm, just barely reaching her toes as she backs into the trees around her. See Nora's eyes raise to the window. See them meet. See Nora's clothes peel like exuviae. Fall around her feet. Hands reach up on her, slide down her arms like knives. She lowers now onto the bed. She is gone from the frame.

We stop for coffee, which we don't need. But I see the other men looking at me and I like it. The girls bounce around the truck stop and everyone watches. I buy them coffee and Doritos and pink sunglasses for Nora.

See the truck from above, a comet, its trajectory a straight white line through the dark.

I was thirteen, I tell them. *I lived in Alaska.* Their wide eyes nod. *It was dark, always. The snowdrifts twenty feet deep. It had been coming around town for several weeks. Killing chickens and cats. Even a horse. I had a gun. I could have frozen to death but I sat through the night. Actually, three. Three nights. I was sitting outside the barn where the horse had been killed just the week before and I sat and I waited and I cocked my gun. He came around the barn and he looked at me. He looked right in my eyes. He was big. Huge. He started pacing me, slowly, one leg crossing in front of the next. He was not going to run. I was scared, wasn't scared. I lifted the gun and pointed it at his snout. I pulled. Clack. Just the tiny click of the hammer. I tried again. It wouldn't even cock. He was still coming toward me. Slowly, no rush. He knew. I rose to my feet and just like that he sprang.* They breathe in. I can see his paws coming at me, claws and fur and the pads of his feet. His mouth snarling yellow behind them. *I grabbed his two front legs. With all my strength I ripped them wide and apart. His mouth smacked against my face, but he was already falling back, already crumpled. I heard his lungs soggy and flapping for breath. His legs dangled. He lay on the snow, blood dripped from his mouth. He raised his head and met my eyes. I knelt beside him and rubbed his ears. I could hear his bones rattling loose as he breathed. Then he stopped.* I stop. *I took him and I hung him from a lamppost in town. Someone took him down. Maybe a bear got him.*

See a boy in dark woods and snow. A stick in his hand. See him wave and stab the stick into the night air. See the monsters crouch and cow. See them run.

Words settle around me. Gather at my feet. *That's not true,* I say. *That's not the worst thing I ever did. It was Marie, that was the worst. That's not the worst,* Ceire says. I say nothing. And her eyes move at me like a bug's, like she sees ten thousand of me at once. I shatter in prisms in her eyes.

See the eyes soaking in. See the eyes flicker like lights. Like moths to light. Vibrating, burning, wings stutter like a flame going out.

Want to know the worst thing I've ever done? says Ceire. *Yes,* I say. I don't. There's something in her eyes. I don't want to know. *She was very old. She was tired and she was old. Sick. She was white and papery. I only had to blow. She would drift away in streamers. Every day she lay in her bed and her flesh flaked more and more and soon she'd be only a page. I only had to blow. Right, Nora?* They snort. *She left the light on,* Nora says. *So I could see.*

See a white head on a pillow. A mouth held open, tongue askew. See a white pillow on a head. See white hands reach up. Paw the air. See white hands claw against arms. See nails on skin, see blood on skin. See blood on the white pillow. See the arms fall. See the white head still. See Nora back into the woods. Pull the hood over her head.

She was sick, Ceire says and it's a whine. It's the voice of a little girl. I turn to look at her and she is—she's a little girl. Blink. She's back. Blink. She's a worm, eyeless and intestinal, propped against the seat. Blink, she's a horned beetle with iridescent shell, blink, a snake, with long eyelashes. Blink. She's back. Ceire. Darkness bleeds down the walls of the cab, down the edges of my vision. I shake my head. Powder drifts like salt to the bottom of my skull. The girls are quiet. Stare straight ahead out the window. I say nothing. The night goes everywhere.

See a flash skirt the highway. A white shape. A blur.

Jeder Engel ist schrecklich, Nora says. Ceire chorts. I nod, unsure. *What language is that?* I ask.

See the white form blur, move. See it slice through the night, see it streak across the road.

White in the road. A deer. A dog. But I see her face. Its face. A moon across the windshield. Eyes meet mine. Scratching brakes on metal. Screeching tires on road. White trailed out behind like smoke, like a dress. The clunk, the crunch, the slurp is sickening. Flesh against steel. There is no way else to say it.

See red lights light up. See the trailer sway like a sail. See tar, two swerving lines lay themselves out on the pavement behind.

I didn't see her. It. I didn't see it. Ceire was in my eye. In the corner of my eye, my eye leaning toward her, trying not to look. My eye leaned away from the road. *I didn't see it*, I say. *I didn't see it.* The girls say nothing. The truck is on the side of the road. The truck is stopped. My hands are shaking. My whole body is shaking. I move to undo my seat belt. My hands are still on the wheel. My hands stuck. I move to undo my seat belt. I do not move. The girls do not move. There is air against my face. The door is open and I am lowering my body to the ground. I watch myself lower. As if I sit outside. As if I still sit in the seat but my body lowers and moves to the ground and moves around the truck and my body circles the truck and my body sees.

See there on the side of the road. See the white heap. A pile of snow. A pile of straw.

I am still frozen. I am still in the truck but the girls are here now. The girls are digging through the pile. The girls are lifting out limbs, legs and fingers wrapped in white rind. The girls are dragging it now. Pulling it from the side of the road and into the fields. Yanking her by the hands and I see her now. Her face. Her small bones. A girl. A young girl and her white gown trails out behind her and what is she doing in that nightdress in the road? Her body carves a path through the grass and I follow and the girls drag the girl and I follow. *There are woods,* they say and I don't see the woods but I follow and soon there are and we are there.

See four bodies, like ants, marched across the stretching fields. See woods inhale them whole.

Ceire takes out a shovel. Where did she get a shovel I almost wonder. My mind floats overhead. My mind sits in the truck and stays warm. *Dig, Gary.* I dig. I dig and dig in a circle around the base of a big tree. I hit roots and I dig around them. I dig through them, slicing them with the blade. The hole is big. It encircles the tree and I don't know how deep it goes. Deep enough. My mind flies away after the light. *That's enough,* they say. *Put her inside,* they say. I look back. The pile in the moonlight. The trees are thick, but a glow breaks through. It halos her face. She is curled like she is asleep. Hair across her forehead. I kneel next to her. Everything inside me runs but I kneel and I look and I wipe back the hair. She is a doll and light blue. She is frozen like snow. I lift her like straw. Lower her into the hole.

See the earth open its mouth. See it lick its lips. See it swallow.

See here, Gary. I look. Nora takes out a gun. Where did she get a gun. And my mind and my thoughts and all my buzzing everywhere charge back together and collide in the bag of my body and suddenly I am only always here. And the gun is pointed at my head. *Now you, Gary.* My eyes move between the girls. Wait for them to smile. Wait for it to stop. I look back at the girl. The dirt around her white dress. *Yes,* one of them says. *Yes.* Their hair is wild in the light. Their legs spread wide. Chests forward. Their mouths twitch. They smile.

See the man. See the man lower to his knees.

I whimper. I wish I could say something else, but I whimper. *It's all going to be okay, Gary,* Nora says, *it's all going to be okay.*

Why. I say. *Why me.* I say. *There are a million little strings,* Nora says. *A zillion invisible threads coming off each of us. Tying everything to everything. You pluck one, and it vibrates. You don't get to know why,* Ceire says.

See the flash. See the bullet as it tears between molecules of air. See the hole torn through the sky. See the bullet cut between cells. See it ripping the web in two.

I want to see your skin off, Ceire says.

See the man, arms and feet tied around the tree. See him curled, like the skeleton of a deer, his bones gray, his fur decaying away.

It's all going to be okay, Gary. It's all going to be okay.

See the girls now lifting, now floating into the sky. See the man there too. See their bodies peel away like wings. Like drops of water, unfold back into an ocean.

Blood on the Moon

I bind my left ankle in a black band to ward off the past; it follows me everywhere. There are bodies, dragging behind me, six, if you count them. Stephen's is the last, the freshest. His teeth clatter as I walk.

They used to bind feet. Now there are high heels. There is a reason Barbie's arches never touch the ground. A reason Achilles' strength waned at the ankle. They understand the power of feet.

The moon is singing to me through the bathroom window. The sliver of pink caught in the medicine cabinet mirror. And it tastes, if song had a taste, like milky bathwater. And it smells of my grandmother. Of course.

I'm brushing my teeth and I'm waiting for him to call. Maybe I'll take a bath. In the dark. In the crescent of the moon. Waxing. Auspicious for putting plans in motion.

She told me, young, of the way the moon tugged at my blood like the tides—how I would be able to tell the future when it was new and cast a man under my spell when she lit my hair blue. I remember that when I plant vegetables that grow in the dark, and someday when a man plants his seed inside mine.

Stephen, I wonder about you as the water washes over the whorls of my nipples. My hands drift to myself and my hair drifts like weeds in the water and the water thickens and the candle flickers in my breath. It feels like a snake shedding its scales under my abdomen and it smells like copper and lemongrass when I come.

I blow out the candle and the phone rings. I know it will be him.

Maxwell arrives and the flowers are cut and pink and I feel their blood streak across my wrist and I see it there in dark red lines although it is clear sap, of course. Hey gorgeous, he says and he brushes the hair from my eyes and I feel the smoothness and I think of Stephen and the rough pads of his fingertips and I wonder how Maxwell will die. And when.

Ten paces from a flowering oak, a hole dug crosswise on the first day of waning will swallow whatever is buried there irretrievably. A stolen earring. A stamped out snake. The past.

We sit on the grass and he pulls food wrapped in plastic from a sack. Sandwiches cased in hard triangle shells. Wine from the bottle. I am charmed by the unromance of it all. He fumbles and his face tries to go hard but it crumbles when he raises his eyes and meets mine. I like a quiet man.

Maxwell is a neighbor. He lives a few houses down from my blue two-story and I met him when I moved in several weeks ago. It's an odd neighborhood and sitting on my stoop in the fading evening the people watching is ideal. I met Maxwell there. I asked him for a light and as I sucked at my joint I could see his eyes widen and his chest lean toward me, just an inch. Venus had recently reversed from retrograde, and he sat with his black and white dog and we watched night slink down into the streets. He asked me out and I said no. But last night he was telling me a story and his dog was nuzzling in his crotch and he was laughing and trying to stay composed and his hair was falling across his face and I told him I would. And I thought maybe he could stand it.

Stephen. Is he the best place to start? He is everywhere, what choice do I have? Teeth rattling in the night. Teeth straight as fence posts. His muscles hard and tattooed. This doesn't make a man strong. I've learned. She was growing in my belly. The moon was still full, but I knew. I felt her the night we made her, felt her cleave to the wall of my insides, felt her swim into shape. He was leaving. The moon hid herself behind the cover of clouds and what light there was felt silver and misted over. I cried onto my pillow and I looked out the window and the night winked at me and the wind blew in my ears. And then there was the clatter of teeth and bones and the sick wet crunch of collapse as skull met concrete. And he was a puddle at the base of the steps. And what could I do but bind him in red rope to keep the jackals away?

The next day my insides were still and I knew she was gone, too.

Maxwell brought chocolate cake and he is looking at me at that angle that I can see down the tunnel of his eyes to the translucent space of his memory, and everything he wants swims too close to the surface and I have to close my eyes at him. He asks if I'm tired. I smile and tell him, no. We walk home and I watch myself rip slowly and carefully in two. Half of me stops at the fence. I invite him into my backyard and we sit under the willow and I light the paper lanterns hanging from the branches. His eyes are fogged and his hair lit from behind. It is lovely beyond what things should be and I know it is too late.

He tells me about his mother and this is early, but I listen and I sweep away into it. Eyes at hip level. An apron and the smell of bread and bluewhite light from a window above our heads. And the tearing away and that is familiar too. I leave his memory and go to my own. She at her dressing table, her long waving hair from the back, the crescent of her eye in the mirror. Tubes and cream for the eyelids, paint for blood in the lips, powder and rouge, bottled smells of petals, of the sea. And the jewels that made her invincible. The gold necklace that could make her fly. The diamond earrings, they took away death. She could live forever. In the mirror on the dresser, pressed into youth behind powder and cream, she would never get old.

It is cloudy in the day of my memory. She has locked me in and left the house. To shop, ostensibly, groceries. I am angry. Anger at the mother is like none other. I wish she were dead. I move to her dressing table. I see myself in the mirror. A full moon rising. I realize, suddenly, by surprise, that I am pretty now. I powder my high nose, rouge my cheeks, color in my translucent lips. I paint myself with the sea, snap gold over my neck and wrists. I pin the diamonds into my ears. I see a red glow lighting around me; I hover off the ground. At the crunch of the garage door my feet sink to the floor. I remove all the jewelry, put her makeup back into place. Run to my room. But I'm forgetting something. I'm hiding the truth. I'm hiding her earring. Just one. Under my tongue. I keep it there until night falls around the house and I go out to the tree in the yard and the moon tells me where and I bury it deep. The soil smells like earthworms and metal, but something else, something surprising, like cotton candy, like spun sugar.

Mother knows what's missing. She knows the chink in her armor. The shouting and the gnashing of teeth, the tail of her fury encircling my neck. But I say nothing.

I see her naked before her mirror one day, me peeking in the slit between the door. Her breasts dragging like bags, pointed nipples cracking and dry, flesh unwinding in rolls down her body.

She begins to fade after this. Her skin grows taut and yellowy over her suddenly crisp bones. Her hair, light like mine, but red too, turns the dulled brown of fall leaves and like the leaves falls in clumps onto the floor, which I sweep as I follow behind her, always trailing her, with a broom. Have you seen someone take her last breath? Have you seen a life leave a body? It is like nothing else. Death is a syringe that sucks out the insides, the organs and the blood and leaves just the dry brittle shell.

But it happens in an instant; it happens while you watch.

Maxwell leans in toward me and I catch his breath in mine. His lips encircle me and my air strangles around his and I hollow him. And it is much too late.

Before Stephen, who was there? I'm not sure I can go in order, it's not how memory works, but there was Leif. I was young and we were swimming in the night. It was hot, it was summer and the noise in the air was crackling, all crickets and swaying branches and first love. And all I really remember is the desire to swallow him, to have his lungs moving against the inside of my cavity always. And our white legs swam under the water and brushed against one another, intertwining like the tentacles of a single organism and I thought it could be like that. I floated on my back and looked at the moon, full and white like it always is when you're young and in love and she smiled, and the sound of water washed through my ears. When I came back to the surface, Leif was gone. The lake took care of the body; there was nothing else to be done.

I awake in the afternoon and begin my preparations. Jojoba oil applied to the lids of my eyes. Ylang-ylang at my pulse points. I rub between my legs and it's sticky wet. I pull out my fingers, painted red, clumps of brown fiber between them. I rub the coagulation against my thumb, spread it across my wrist where it balls and dries into a film. Mark a red x. I light my apartment with candles in the sun and wash the wood floors with vinegar and lemon. I chop garlic and onion—my eyes water—then simmer them in oil with oregano and thyme. From the mason jars lining the pantry I find the summer's Old Virginia tomatoes, sweet from the cool June nights and crush them into the pot. The sauce bubbles and spits and I dice the carrots and salt the meat. My hair curls in the steam. In the bathroom, I line my eyes with black and put on a long yellow dress, gold bangles on my wrists and a single diamond in my ear. The light is congealing, preparing to set, pinking the room. There is a buzzing at the door.

If you skin a snake, in the morning someone will die. I've learned. I didn't know him, but there he was, laid crosswise on the steps. He smelt of piss and homelessness. His early aged face peaceful and gray. A clean gash down the center of his chest, ribcage cracked, heart intact. I smudged him with sage before the police arrived, unsure of how much responsibility to bear.

Daddy died before I was born. He doesn't count, I don't think, my daddy. He rattles along behind Mother.

For centuries my uterus was drawn with horns. Hell was a womb, demons spawned inside.

He wipes his bloody mouth. Smiles at me. Our eyes drop to our dinner. He starts to talk. I don't know why he wants to open like this. But he does. Peels back the boney thorax like a rolling cabinet and it's soup inside.

"There's something about you," he says, "that's untainted." And I laugh. "No," he continues, "there's something in you untouched by this world."

"There is something in you that's a mirror," I say.

I packed my suitcase. Not much, just a few dresses, my jewelry, the cat. He caught me at the stairs. He'd always had a temper. I should have known by his hitchhiker's thumb. This was Harrison. Shadowed, in all ways. But it was that, the swirling nightmare inside him, and the silent space at its center—that was it. He caught me at the top of the stairs and dragged me by my wrists, twisting my arms, my suitcase dropping down the well. I remember the sound, the hollow chunk. The cat gone from my arms. I slapped him across the mouth; I remember that sound too, the solid, dank lurch of flesh. I don't remember the next sound, just the impact and the blackening floor as my head descended toward it.

I awoke, how many days, how many lifetimes later? A needle lay on the floor next to me. My arms were scabbed. My wrists tied to the radiator with the curtains. Harrison sat in the only chair, the recliner, on the other side of the room. He looked out the window. Faded in the light. I called to him. Baby, please, I'm sorry. By the time I had the knots loosened I already knew. I didn't need to see the glass in his eyes. My suitcase was still in the stairwell. Clothes scattered. The cat was nowhere. I gathered my belongings. I left. Whatever might come for him had already been there, and gone. For whatever humanness there might have been left to take.

Maxwell stands and grabs my hand and in his eyes there is something new. He leads me to the bedroom, behind a curtain on the other side of the kitchen, and presses my body between his and the wall. His tongue curls over mine, down my neck, to my collarbone and I dig my fingers into his hair. I pull and his neck pulls back and he looks right into me. I shut against it and feel his mouth, hot, move to my breast.

The first person I ever knew die was Lacey Thompson. Lacey left sixth grade after the story circulated that she had let three guys stick their fingers in her in the ball closet of the gymnasium. She told the principal that they'd held her in there, that they'd pinned her down. But the story that circulated was she'd told them to meet her there, let them do it, one version even involved a broomstick, and she'd asked for it. Even the gym teacher said so. Lacey transferred. I laughed, with the others. Called her slut. One of the boys won some award for citizenship that year. Have you heard that urban legend about the girl who committed suicide with a broomstick? Why is it always a broomstick? Where she jumps off the table? That's not what Lacey did. Hers was a bridge. But still, the thought makes my insides shiver.

I was with Lacey Thompson on the bridge. I stood behind her. Her feet toed the edge of the planks. She wavered, forward then back. I blew on the back of her neck.

Sometimes I see them, in the blanks of my peripheral vision. Lacey's blond hair is laced with seaweed and her skin is nearly blue. Her mouth is a gaping hole. And sometimes I hear her moan.

On the night she turns thirteen, the snake uncoils and bites the girl, and from the two fang holes in her neck she bleeds. And like the snake, for the rest of her days she'll shed her cells, and like the snake, she never dies.

The room is humid, a microclimate of our breath, and his fingertips trace me like a paper doll along the perforations and when he slips inside of me I slip out of the night. La petite mort, and I laugh.

I grow scales and fat lizard thighs. My cunt splits and births a tongue. A fish with great teeth swims inside.

Maxwell sleeps and his breath is shallow and I wonder if it's even there. With red lipstick, I paint an x on each ankle and each wrist. I will keep vigil until morning. I watch the moon redden in her arc across the sky as it lightens. The edges of my vision shake. Heaviness seeps into my limbs and it becomes dark, my eyes roll from my head.

♦

I am flattened like a snake and emptied of voices, the letters of their names fill my wide mouth. When they find me they will cut me open and out they will spill, all of them. They will slice through to the sack of my mother's uterus, and within Lamia's belly, the bones will knock.

On the Thinness of Skin

"Do you want white legs or black?"

"What's the difference?" Nora asked, rubbing her hand over the loose sheath of the pale knee as it batted against the chair she sat in. The Madam stood over her, several pairs on hangers over her wrist.

"One's white, one's black."

Nora looked up to where the Madam stood, she met her eye and held it. It was deep green, rimmed in crusting liner and soft, papered wrinkles. The woman held the gaze back, accustomed, then lifted her shoulders and smiled lightly.

"Well, there's the tone, of course, muscle structure, and texture, hair or hairlessness, but—" and with this the Madam's eyelids fluttered, "and this is most important: the legs are the house of the sex, the libido. An important choice."

Nora paused, adjusted her feet on the frayed Turkish rug. She leaned forward, trying to get a better view of the bodies hanging in rows behind the Madam. Came back to the Madam's eyes.

"Which is most popular?" she asked.

Again the green eyes bore into her, unpacking boxes in her skull. A pause, and then the shoulders lightened and the smile lifted like before.

"Clever girl." A laugh burst from the Madam's lips. "Well it's not what you might expect—of course the black ones are more sexual, hypercharged, but that's not what all men want. Many love the 'white angel,' the prying apart at the knees—"

Nora laughed, "Oh fuck off it, Madam. I'm not a John. Do they really fall for that?" She laughed again. "You know better than anyone that's not real. Shite, they're dumb. As they wanta be. But, I mean, what about each person, how does each individual bring her own essence? How do I choose which girl I want?"

Madam laughed back, a low boil in her throat. "Stupid girl. Where do you think you are? This is not the land of the real. This is the land of image. *Real*?" She laughed again, a higher pitch. "There is no individual essence," she said, her cataract eyes locking on Nora, the laughter gone.

Nora looked away. "I'll take the black legs," she said.

Madam pressed a button and the hanging racks lurched forward. Dozens of legskins in varying shades of brown swung back and forth as if blown in a wind. Tufts of hair at every crotch.

"Would you like grooming? $30–60 extra, depending."

"I'll take it as it is," Nora said, "but don't I get to choose the pair?"

Madam snapped a pair of legs from the rack and her gaze closed off. "I already told you, the individual doesn't matter, they're all the same. We could spend all day, you here flipping through legs. I choose." Madam hung a pair on the empty bar beside the chair, rapped cracked fingernails on the brass. "The Johns don't complain, they don't care," she added.

"I do," said Nora. "I'm not a John."

"You're not paying full price. Now for the torso," said Madam, "what size would you like?"

Nora scanned the windowless backroom, a place—actually located in the high-ceilinged basement beneath The Picture House—she'd never been before. Madam usually met customers in the lounge on the first floor, took their orders and returned a half hour later with a girl. When Nora used to drop off parts, she would meet Buzz, the big bouncer-like fellow with a mean stare but a soft peach fuzz under his chin, giving him a childlike feel when you got close, in a sanitized cellar—the kitchen they called it, a small room with metal floors, walls and counters, probably just behind this room now that she thought about it—that opened into the alley behind the House. This backroom a strange imbalance, the faded rugs and curtains, the deep flesh tones of the rooms upstairs, in uncomfortable contrast to the metal and motors of the factory equipment.

"What about my hands?" Nora asked.

"Eh? How could you use your own hands?"

"No, I mean you used to say that they requested my hands, asked special for them," Nora said.

"Ah, those hands," said Madam, reaching, unconsciously perhaps, to the chair arm and taking one of Nora's hands into hers. The hand flipped instinctively over, lying belly up and soft like a fish between the wrinkled skin. The Madam's breathing slowed, rasped; she smiled lightly. After a moment, Nora's hand readjusted its direction and her fingers slipped between the ones encaging them, softening against the film around them, vibrating, an imperceptible pulse passing between them. Madam's eyes fell closed, her head dropped back on her neck, a minute passed. Then she rolled back into place, eyes opened, clucked her mouth at Nora and dropped her hand. "Those hands," she whispered, touching her face.

She shook her head against its blurriness. "The torso," Madam said and flipped a small silver lever on the panel behind her. The hanger bar croaked, as if under a heavier load, but the torsos when they arrived were skin, loose and slack like the legs.

"The weight of the heart," Madam noted.

"You said there was no individual—"

"What size?"

"Then why did they ask for my hands?"

Madam shook, slightly, as if drying herself of something and said nothing.

Nora grazed her eyes over the bodies. Rows reaching back farther than she could see. "What's that over there?" she asked, leaning so far forward she spilled out of the chair. She pointed to a dark corner across from the mechanical clothing racks, where it looked like several people were propped against the back wall. Madam spun and looked.

"Oh. Those are permanents," she said. "They're always here. And they come as-is, pre-built. They're discount."

"Permanent?" Nora asked. "Like their owners never pick them up?"

"Like their owners never leave."

"They're still there? Still inside?" The silence that followed began to suffocate her.

"No," said the Madam. "What size torso? Extra small to double XL."

"But where do they go?" Nora said. "Where do their selves stay?"

The Madam heaved a breath and rolled her eyes back at the bodies before turning again to Nora. "Down to the bottom," she said, "feet and ankles, sometimes the toes."

Nora looked at her a moment. "I think I'd like one of those," she said.

"We're nearly done with your personal! Those are completely uncustomizable."

"I'll take one," Nora said. "I'll take that one on the left, with the curly hair."

"She's not like you," Madam said. "She's not at all like you. You said you wanted yourself." Madam rubbed the pads of her thumbs against her nails. "I don't judge. I just provide the girls. But that's what you said."

"I'll take her," Nora said, and pointed again.

Madam turned and sighed deep and overloudly and repeatedly as she recalled hanging rows of bodies with a whir and returned the legs to the rack and lined the flat-heeled, paintless feet back onto the rolling belt where they were carried away through a small hole in the wall. "Stupid girl," she muttered.

Nora watched, distractedly, but her eyes kept returning to the permanent, to the body against the wall. Madam ducked beneath a row of clacking ribcages and pulled the body out by its hair. It was big, but it dragged limp and flaccid across the carpet.

She lifted it up before Nora, the jaw hanging slack, the eyelids peeled back, brown eyes blank. Nora jumped back a little even though she was prepared, still slightly knocked askew by the combined absence and presence of life.

"This the one you want?" Madam asked.

After Madam had dragged the girl behind the bulky purple drapes and Nora plugged her ears against the sound like electric screaming and the air had taken on that smell of a lightning storm, with just a tinge of singed hair, Nora and the girl—Noreen she'd called her when Madam told her she needed to be named to turn on—lowered onto the worn velvet seats of the brass elevator and watched the arrow at the top count the ascending floors.

"If it doesn't depend on individual character," Nora had asked before Madam made Noreen alive, "how does it work with the permanents? How are they determined?"

"The buyer determines the content," Madam replied, and here her eyes gentled. "Surely you know that about this line of work by now, child."

The elevator stopped at the seventh floor. Noreen followed Nora down the dim-lit hall to the fourth door, marked with the number etched into wood. Against the darkly painted wall of the small room stood a brass bed covered with a hand-knit blanket and pillow, feathers poking from its corners.

She sat on the threadbare bed and looked at herself. No, Nora thought, Madam was right, this was not her. But the permanent, the girl, Noreen, sat, like a fish behind a bowl, examined. Light fell in through the thin pink curtains, though it was nearly night, and brushed across Noreen's broad legs and bare feet. Nora raised her hand at a right angle to her body. Noreen didn't move.

"Follow me," Nora said. "Haven't they trained you at all?" she asked, suddenly very angry. She grabbed the girl's wrist and tore it into the air, to the position hers had been in before, stuck out straight like a scarecrow. Noreen held it there when Nora took her hand away.

"Do you feel pain?" Nora asked.

Noreen looked at her. Nora pinched her forearm, hard and deep as she remembered her mother sometimes doing to her as a child. Noreen flinched. She did not cry out. Nora felt immediately sorry. She kissed Noreen on the spot and sat again opposite her on the bed. They stared at each other. Noreen held her gaze, her brown eyes, feathered with light, nearly blonde lashes, vacant empty glass, but moving—vibrating and processing.

"Talk," Nora said. "Tell me your name."

"Noreen," the permanent answered. In a voice, a human voice—a timber, a distinction—but hollow at its center. Noreen's arm still stood out at her side.

"Put your arm down," Nora said.

The arm across from her lowered. Nora leaned her head to her right, her light hair brushing her bony shoulder. Noreen mimicked, her curly brown hair dangling down over her wide bicep. Nora straightened her head. Noreen did the same.

"Better," Nora said.

They looked at each other a long while, a dim crackling in the air between them. Finally, Nora stood from the bed and smoothed the bottom of her short white dress and then lifted it quickly over her head. She stood in her torn maroon stockings, which pinched slightly her soft waist, and black laced bra, covering her small and rounded breasts. Noreen stood and did the same, pulling up the green dressing gown Madam had dressed her in. She was naked underneath. Round folds of her flesh settling down upon one another.

"You are beautiful," Nora said, her mouth puckering like a sneer.

Noreen looked back at her, not in the same way, not a peering, a prodding at the body, but only a met gaze. The bed between them, Nora reached out her hand straight ahead, toward Noreen.

Noreen paused, and then reached back, her left arm moving for Nora's right. Their fingers didn't reach, inches of space flared out between them, and then Nora dropped both hands to the bed and kneeling onto her haunches began to crawl across. Noreen waited on the other side. Her arm still outreached.

Nora lifted her head under Noreen's hand and rubbed against it like a pet. The girl's hand flattened against the pressure, and then pressed back lightly, curving gently to scratch and rub. Her fingers dug into the hair, peeling it back into rivets. Nora closed her eyes and felt like earth, canyons and streams torn and divided into her skull by god. She did not intend to moan but did not stop herself. Nora lowered to the bed when she was finished, her tights damp between her legs and let the warmth in her chest exhale.

She lay there, her eyes closed, and felt Noreen settle down beside her. Then she felt her mouth on her neck, her face, the tongue tracing the outline of her, then hands, on her neck, encircling. They grew tight and the mouth was heavy on her mouth, the tongue pressing now inside of her, the bumpy places of her cheeks, deep into the back of her throat, it softening in conditioned reflex. But this was not the way she wanted it. Nora pushed Noreen off, pushed her back, her chest lifting and falling with quickness, and looked at the calm, vacant girl.

Then Noreen's eyes shook, just a little, as if she were calculating, and she said, "What do you want?" And the voice was strange, as if it did not belong to the soft body in front of her and Nora wondered if Madam had added it separately and what would that mean for Noreen, because despite Madam's protestations she knew of course that she was in there still, just as Nora could feel her hands—and sometimes her arms, torso and neck when money was especially tight—or the ghostlike tingling of them, even when she was not in the room where they were.

"Don't say anything," Nora said.

She pushed Noreen further, onto her back, and climbed on top. Again Noreen's dark eyes revealed nothing, batted their blonde eyelashes without sound.

"Lay your head down," she said.

Nora straddled the girl, rising high in the bed on her round belly. She rubbed her moistness against Noreen's navel, hard and fast, like when she was a little girl against the coffee table corner. But it was still not what she wanted. Tears filled her eyes and she slapped them away, then slapped Noreen's freckled cheeks. One after the other, left, right, left, right, left.

She pulled back, down Noreen's legs and feet, dragging herself along the bones, and it felt good but not right still and when she reached the end of the bed she climbed off and stood at its foot. Her breath came too fast, like it was outside of her, dragging her along and tears kept coming to her eyes.

She grabbed Noreen's ankles and pulled them wider; the legs accommodated her without resistance. She went to the drawers and took out four of the leather cuffs, and locked each of the girl's limbs loosely to the brass posts of the bed.

She looked for a long time at the body laid out in front of her. The way the knees bent slightly inward, the curl of the smallest toe, heavy breasts sliding to the sides, dark nipples' indistinct edges fading out in tiny dots, a stray dark hair curling up. She looked at the body laid out before her and had that strange prickly sensation, like her hands working up the shaft of a man, feeling him pull in and against her while she read books in the library. But in the body now, in Noreen's body before her, she saw something like a flicker of her own bones in there and she closed her eyes tight against it. She felt her hands go to work, as if they were detached from her again, as if they were sewn onto another body and she struggled against it, struggled to rein them.

"I am in control," she said aloud.

Noreen's legs widened, and stretched a little, spread slowly apart revealing the curl of her clit, slightly left as if leaning against the thicker lip for support. It was brownish red, lightly purpled on the edges and pressing against the skin around it as it swelled, climbing out. The hair was long and unkempt, dark and slightly matted, collecting moisture in the places where it dipped against the whorl of vagina opening beneath it, shuddering a little, as if with breath.

Nora's hands slid up Noreen's legs, pulling the muscles as they went, lifting the fat from the bone and rolling it like dough and Nora didn't know if she led or if they did and at any rate she didn't care anymore. Noreen groaned, cow-like, as the hands reached her thighs but they did not speed up, the hands, as they moved all around from front to back, bottom to top.

They slid onto her pubic mound and pulled deeply in the hair, rubbing it as the girl had rubbed Nora's head earlier, stretching it as if to braid and raising gently up the skin beneath. Noreen was moaning consistently now, rocking back and forth ever so slightly in her hands.

Two fingers dropped down around the clit, squeezing it between them like a mouse stuck in a closing door. Noreen gasped, her breathing heightened, her moans going higher pitched as the fingers slipped back and forth around the button, then the fingers rose onto their tips to circle the whole clit strip, out to the edges of the lips, back to the button head and around, again and again. The other hand reached up to the asshole, pressing fingers lightly against its closed edges like a doorbell, watching it tighten and then release with each pump. Pressing harder sometimes, slipping inside.

Now the picture came, a bird beating its wings, the cage brass and sharp.

Nora and Noreen both wheezing and moaning hard, deeper now, and when she lowered her tongue and tasted the salt and copper and sour tang, everything let go, viscous and wet all over her mouth.

As Noreen shook, Nora's hands moved up her body, pushing into the folds of her belly, stretching apart the flesh at her navel and admiring the shape, the puffed circle, folded at the center. She moved her hands to Noreen's large breasts and cupped them, sliding them from the edges of her body where they'd dropped, to the center, seamlessly dragging each finger across the nipple, one at a time, just enough to make contact as it hardened and rose. She put a nipple in her mouth, trying to encircle the wide areola, and then began to suck earnestly. Noreen neither moaned nor cried out until there was a tightening in the breast and sweet milk began to flow. Nora sucked both breasts dry, then unlocked the four cuffs and curled up alongside the woman.

"Where do you come from?" Nora asked as she lay down beside her.

Noreen's hair was brittle and streaked white as Nora passed her hands through it, tangling in the curls. She rolled to the side and Nora traced the lines down her neck and onto her chest, between the empty sacks dragging to the bed.

"From over there," Noreen answered, the voice still young and strange, her fingers flicking in some direction.

"Me too," Nora said.

It was quiet.

"Hold me," Nora said and Noreen laid her body, narrowing now, around Nora and after a few moments she couldn't breathe.

She pushed back and looked in Noreen's face, the eyes yellowing, the parchment ripped through with wrinkles and unspeakably thin.

"I have to get you out of here," Nora said, suddenly jumping up.

She went to the window, pulled back the curtains and the glass and reached out into the now orange air. "Come," she told Noreen, "come here now."

Noreen had trouble rising from the bed, her bones rickety and bent.

"Give me this," Nora said and her hand wrapped around Noreen's sex, dry and crinkled now, and ripped it out, vulva and organs and all. In the empty space dangled tendons and tubes and torn layers of dermis. She swaddled it in her white dress which it quickly stained dark, and put the bundle under the pillow.

"Come now," Nora said gently and lifted the old lady onto the sill.

Nora's and Noreen's eyes locked and the vacancy was gone.

Nora placed a hand on each side of Noreen's face, cupped the cheeks. Then she pushed, softly, and the body fell backward and out, upturned feet the last thing to disappear out of the frame.

Nora did not look out the window at the body spread across the sidewalk below, the blood sprayed out like feathers alongside.

Emptied

Nora woke and the pain in her leg was not gone. If anything, it was worse. The failure of the medicine pressed her like weight to the bed. The state of her heart was no better either, but in the pale light of morning it was less acute, pain being always harder to stomach in the bright sun. She woke and it was again with the picture of a desert thorn tree growing on the plateau of a high mountain. She was not asleep, the image held under her waking eyelids, but it was crystallized and sharp as a dream and she knew she had to leave him.

The boy, the man, but he was still a boy—just as Nora was still a girl though her body and her years and her desires were not—had latched himself to a hook inside the cavity of her chest. He was trying to be a writer and sometimes he would give her what he thought were pieces of himself cloaked in words, but they were not pieces of himself. They were only words, with empty space in between.

When she had been a girl, she had loved another girl and girls are cruel, crueler than boys but only because they have that inner vision to see the softest places, the holes in a person's shell that go straight through to the unprotected parts and before they are women and they learn better, they will poke it and the soul will shake. Nora could see the holes in the boy the same as she could see the freckles on his back or the scar on his neck but she would not poke them. Even when he pulled with all his strength against the place he had hooked insider her and ripped at her walls, she would not scratch him. She had poked at a man before and the shivering had been more than she could stand.

Nora worked as a seamstress and there was something in that, in connecting things to cover or carry or wear, in stitching skins. But still work felt like that, like a coat she had sewn and draped over her skeleton, like something that was neither a part of her nor this life, but something she had to put on to keep warm.

The holes she saw in the boy, the glimpses she got, were between panels of wood nailed over one another in a haphazard way. A maze of tight hallways and doors opening onto nothing. Layers meant to evade and confuse but it wasn't hard to find her way. There were bits of light and her sense was especially strong.

But she always loved men like that.

She bent her knee against her chest and pressed her fingers into the small indentations running lengthwise up her calf. She couldn't bring herself to look, from fatigue or fear she wasn't sure. There were more, certainly, they reached nearly to her knee. She started where they began at her ankle and counted up, twenty-seven marks. Yesterday there had been twenty-five. She should go back to the clinic.

She flung her feet to the edge of the bed as if to rise, but changed her mind and flapped the covers back over herself instead. *Lifting sheets snap air across the room, dust motes and some buried scent of him hover in a shape, then disperse.* Her chest tightened in reflex and her sternum pushed closer and it was hard to breathe.

She pulled herself from bed some hours later and the sun was clothed in clouds and it looked like rain and she was grateful.

She watched herself in the full-length mirror as the shower warmed and fog filled in around her. Reflections always seemed to her to be violent—inverse cutaways of the solid shape on the other side. Her hair hung limp around her face, her dull face, dusted with a powder of ground bones and tinted blue, veins pressing through the skin. She pulled off the robe with remorse. Bones jutted through, her breasts barely bigger than the ribs below them. She turned her leg and looked, the marks creeping up. She measured them the day she noticed there were more, that more appeared every morning; it must have been the third or fourth day after she'd first found them, the day the pain started. The marks were uniformly a half-centimeter in width, length and depth, and arranged in a nearly perfect straight line. They looked like a pockmarked zipper. They looked like pillow marks on your cheek and they burned like ash.

Today she was upholstering a couch, which was not really her work, but her friend Colleen's. But she helped and the fabric was turquoise and wool and the wood dark and full of smells and she knew there was magic in making this. Like maybe somewhere else she was covered in something just like it. Colleen's hair was long and black and dull, her cheeks ruddy, her eyes hazel and horse-lidded. She looked like each part of her was taken from another person and pasted into a collage. She was startlingly beautiful.

Colleen's hands worked like snakes and Nora was telling her about the vision of the thorn tree.

"What color is the dirt?"

"The dirt? Brown. Well, reddish, I guess."

"Mm-hmm." Colleen nodded. "Describe it, all of it."

"The leaves are sage, like light green, kind of bushy, but thin. The dirt is like those pictures of the desert when the sun is setting, glowing orange or red. I can see the trunk clearly. It's brown and gray. It curves, twists; it's knotted, fibrous, like it's almost dead, like you could peel pieces away. And I'm coiled inside."

"You can see yourself?"

"Well, I know it's me. It's not like I see my body, but I see that I'm there inside the tree, or I just know."

"And there is only one tree?"

"Yes, hanging off the edge of the cliff."

Nora held the fabric folded against the wood molding. Colleen's hair hung in her eyes and she wove her hands through the air, pinning fabric with nails, which she held between her lips as she mumbled.

"A Joshua tree," Colleen said. "It means you should turn toward your future."

Nora snorted, wiped the snot that shot from her nose.

Colleen closed her eyes, "It's true—that's why it's twisted; it's reaching."

Nora laughed again.

"I'm serious. Don't be a bitch, Nora."

Nora smiled at her friend. They worked in silence.

"How's your leg?"

"Better," Nora lied.

Colleen was quiet and dug at Nora with her gaze. "You look like shit," she said finally.

The man, the boy had taken her to the clinic. Both the first time and last week, to get her leg examined. But his face was lined with wood and he'd looked past her—he'd already pulled away, is what that meant. She tried for a while to chase him but got lost in the torn up branches. He'd carved new tunnels, put up new boards, and the hook in her chest ached. The doctors didn't say much. They gave her some cream for psoriasis and some pain meds. She couldn't ask for much more. She had no insurance. It had nothing to do with the procedure, they assured her. She turned to look at him as they were leaving that last time. Trapped his face in hers. The light brown pupils, the bent nose. His eyes retracted several inches into his head. His cheek twitched. He smiled, grabbed her hand, and spun her around.

Nora and Colleen went to lunch and Nora ate heavily.

"He's emptying you," Colleen said and Nora laughed. "No," she continued, "that's it. He's sucking the life out of you."

"Is he chewing up my leg too?" she asked. "And when, I'd like to know; I haven't seen him in two weeks."

"You don't have to see him. You've connected yourself to him. You have to cut the cord, close the channel. Breaking it off is not enough," Colleen said throwing bits of fried chicken skin across the table with emphasis.

"Jesus, Colleen. Can we just eat?"

"Fucking vampire," she muttered.

They sat in silence. Colleen drinking her tea. Nora stared out the window. *The air beside them gels, and flickers or lightens for a second, and then it is gone.*

The pins stuck like antennae from the white body and it twirled in the window in the harsh light. She was hemming a dress when the boy knocked at her door.

He kissed her and made his way to the couch. She sat beside him. They looked at each other's knees. "How have you been?" she asked. He caught the question in his teeth and pressed his mouth against hers. He leaned her back. He wrapped her legs around his waist and carried her onto the bed.

There was something about their sex and it was in the way she inhaled him, absorbed him almost. She opened with him not in the usual sense but became boundaryless, her cutis porous and unprotective. He drained into her—she could almost see him pass, pour in like she was sieved. When they were happy it had filled her, this part of their sex like this, stretched her to the edges of the space she took up in the world. But now it hollowed her. Now it was like being full of ether—of cold, ghostly nothing.

The truth was, she hadn't wanted the baby. But it was here regardless. The air just behind her or sometimes inside the crook of her arm was charged, opaque or glowing it was hard to say—it was just there, just always outside of seeing. *And now it lies in the bed between them, a glistering space.* Now that it was here, she just wanted to feed it, to open like a jar of milk. The boy's breath heaved and his chest rose and fell and his soul spread out through his nose and filled the room.

She knew if she fell asleep they would all three dissolve, so she kept her eyes open as long as she could. Already the man was exiting his solid shape and the baby didn't have one and once her consciousness shut down and no one was there to see they would seep, the three, into a soup of waves and particles. She must stay awake here to keep them all in place.

He kissed her in the morning, while she was still partly asleep, his solidity slamming back together in her vision, careening continental plates. And then he was gone. His absence still bright above her bed. She got up and ignored the pain. She got up and went to the grocery store to feel that she was still a part of this world.

On the bus, she leaned her face against the window and when it rocked her head would bounce and smack against the glass. It kept her from falling asleep. She opened her eyes. There was a crazy bus lady sitting across from her. There is always a crazy bus lady. The woman plucked things from her bags and arranged them on the seats next to her. Strange bundles of dirty cloth. It took Nora a minute to realize the things were dolls. They were made of rags or rope or metal pieces. She squinted. One looked like balled up newspaper with masking tape. Another had a real head, a plastic doll head with full blond hair and one eye. One looked like a T-shirt, rolled and tied, a silver washer around its neck. The lady continued pulling out dolls, arranging them next to her until at last she must have emptied them all and she folded her arms over her swollen belly and leaned back her head and smiled. Nora leaned back too and closed her eyes again. She opened them when she felt something in front of her. The woman's face hovered over hers, slack lips spittled with balls of saliva only inches from her own. The fine check-marked lines of skin cells fitting together, the glaze of sweat, the cheek pores microscoped at close range.

"I smell it on you," the woman said, her too-thick tongue spilling from her mouth. "You're putrefying inside." She cackled and fell back into her seat, folded her arms again and gazed serenely at Nora until she got off.

Everything in the store seemed oversized under the strange greenish light. The boxes of food lining the shelves, the people with their slow-moving hands and giant mouths. Like she was shrinking and dulling, everything around her scintillating and loud. The frozen food aisle was so cold and she could stand in front of the doors, her bones nearly chattering, for long minutes and no one would say anything. She pressed her face against the glass and let it creep across her, that feeling of cold like she had detached and floated around outer space, connected only by a rope, and an oxygen tank. The store wasn't working. *She walks the aisles, a cord dragging down between her legs, the baby skidding behind on the white tile.* She kneeled in front of the sugary cereal. The colors, the bright cartoon faces swirling in spirals. She might pass out. A little child sat beside her. It was hard to tell if it was a boy or girl. A stringy bowl cut, light hair, black eyes. The child wrinkled its nose. Nora wrinkled back. The child reached out and touched her hair. She closed her eyes. Its touch blurring the air between them. She knew if she spoke it would shatter, the sea around impassible with language. She heard a noise, a name and felt the child running away. But its hand stayed there in her hair. She was afraid to open her eyes. Afraid of the faces, rainbow bright colors. Without the solid flesh of the child to keep her planted. Her phone buzzed in her pocket. It was Colleen.

"Pick me up," Nora said. "I might be dying."

She woke up several hours later in bed. Colleen rubbed oil on the marks on her leg. They crawled up over her knee now.

"I've been googling," Colleen said. "These herbs are for parasites and skin infections, and this oil is antiseptic and moisturizing."

Nora smiled at her. It was weak. *The air in the room is bright and somehow glistening, like it is wet.* And they both pretended not to notice. Nora tried not to see her reflection in Colleen's face, the droop of her eyelids signifying fear. It might cut her away, a mirror like that. It might erase her.

"I called the douchebag three times," Colleen said. "He's not answering."

They watched a movie and Nora half slept.

In the night Nora started coughing, a cough like something tearing out, like lungs splitting open.

♦

Nora pushed through the darkened door. Sand red and hot. Dunes rolling out from under her in waves. A thorn tree in the distance. She squinted against the white sun. She scraped her soles along the ground as it gave beneath her, lifted onto her toes to push away from the heat. She looked down at her legs, at the exposed flesh, at the jagged lines of muscle, darker than the ground below them. She heard a noise and raised her gaze out into the distance. From behind the mounds, red figures were moving, coming toward her now. They formed into humans or carcasses as they moved into her range of sight. Muscles stripped of dermis, striated lines of maroon and pink, leathered shells in the bright light—yellow tendons stretching like rubber bands as they walked. And when they were close enough to touch her, the bloodied strips of their mouths lifted into smiles. There were adult bodies and children and some of them held small bundles. One reached out its sinewed arms, passing Nora a wriggling hulk. She opened instinctively and pulled it toward her. The meat moved. The baby looked up, its unbound eyeballs rolling up to meet hers, the levators lifting the corners of its mouth into a twist. She dropped it to the ground.

The Baby in the Bottle

The baby in the bottle is crying. The baby in the bottle has been crying for days. Maybe forever. You can put a cork in the bottle. But cork breathes. Cork transmits sounds like vibrations across your bumped skin. The sounds through the cork reach out and pull up the hairs of your arms when the baby screams. The baby screams when the cork is in. It's better, really, to uncork the bottle.

She brought the bottle and she left it on my porch one day. The woman across the street with the red hair and the red apron and no children of her own. It's yours, she said. You dropped it. And now the baby in the bottle is yours.

He's cute to look at when he's sleeping, floating atop the fizzed-out soda pop. Sometimes you call him "she." When it takes your fancy. Or just, "baby in the bottle." The thing is, you've always been alone in this room up here and now you never are, never alone.

The baby in the bottle is crying. You set her on the window-sill. The soda evaporates in the sun and she gets sticky and you think she likes to look at the cars passing below. And one day, a man shows up, and it gets tricky. The man brings flowers and the flowers are pink and you put one in the bottle and she sucks at its stem. And its stem sucks at the coke around her and pulls it up into its leaves, just like a woman, and the leaves turn brown. And the coke is gone and the baby is crying so you fill the bottle with water and now she is happy and quiet in the sun on the windowsill with another pink flower poking out. And the man fills your bed with heat and the smell of fires or just wood or something dark and sweet like evaporated coke and all the stars shine through the window. And she is quiet now. And almost forgotten. When you are alone she is still there. The man, did I tell you what he looked like? His eyes are like pine needles and his laugh reaches down to the bone. His hands are smooth and always hot.

The baby in the bottle is crying—it scrapes your spine when the man leaves your bed and it is cold. Into the bright night he goes. You thought, when you were small, held in the palm of your mother's hand, that the stars were holes and you were so small you might slip through. You were probably right. What now? Now the man is quiet, and the baby, and you are still all alone. But the stars are so loud. The stars are screaming and don't they sound like rushing blood.

The baby has outgrown her bottle and now she's in your bed. The baby has eaten her bottle. Chewed through with razor teeth and the shards are everywhere. Be careful when you roll over, when you step. She lays in bed, swathed in gauze after all those years in glass so she doesn't fall and split her head. Swimming around so you never sleep. And the man? The man? I feel his warm spot still. He must be here somewhere. You could leave too, if you want. But I doubt you will. These walls are your home.

The man, when he puts his hand inside of you and there are a thousand bottles that rattle and clank and then break into a thousand pieces and the blood drips down your leg, licks it away. And you are still alone.

Womb Feather Bone

Big gaps of time and space horrified Nora. Even in the day. If she had too much time between appointments she might find herself in the deepest part of the couch, huddled, unable to move her legs or fully inhale. If, on an unlucky trip into town, the sidewalk emptied and it was suddenly just her in the expanse of concrete and sun, she could remain there for a long stretching rope of minutes, willing her feet to inch forward, battling the disquiet weighting down her shoes.

Perhaps, if she were pregnant, she thought, she would never be alone. But being alone with a man was almost the same as being all alone. So she began to invite them in packs onto her crowded living room couches and sit them among the doilies on the faded green velour. She was not unattractive with her long straight nose and arching brows and had little trouble collecting them. They shifted funnily in their seats, their eyes following her calculated circling of the woven round rug like a cat, until she'd curl up in a corner on the floor. Without word they'd come to her there, one at a time, the others leaning in closer to fill the space with breath and drown out noise.

In the circle, with their heads cocked in and their eyes blinking open and shut, and when she came, Nora saw the big bang pour out of the loop of a vagina and faces flickered as gaseous stars and sound became matter. There was a smell and it was her childhood. The linty electric scent left behind by a vacuum and she inhaled and pulled the sperm up and toward her belly.

Her trash cans filled with pregnancy tests until one day she stopped. There was one man, with soft hair and Nora began to hope he would be the father but he was not.

She walked up and down the sidewalk of her block, and the women with the scarves on their heads watched her and reached out to brush her hair whenever she passed. It was summer and there were many people in the street and the light was almost always red-tinted and she would walk late into the evening. One day in the road, Nora watched two bees. One bee hovering over the smashed body of another. It would fly away and then return, circling the other, sometimes landing atop it. She knelt and watched it for slow minutes. She could not decide if it was grieving its dead friend or eating it. The bees reminded her of a dog she'd had. She had found him in the wood behind the street, which she never walked in even though it was crowded with trees, but one day she wanted to stretch herself, so she did and she found the dog. He was black with a white eye patch and pointed furry ears. Nora took him home because he seemed willing to come and also she desired to bathe with him. He stayed with her and if she would wake in the night he always sat, ears up, paws across her feet, alert and watching her. When she realized that the terror remained, even with him whining and nipping at her feet, she took him back to the wood and left him. She didn't open the door for three days when he followed her home, and then he left.

She knew that there was sadness at the center of everything. Like a little bell it rang, at a very high pitch, at the tune of water. She could hear it. It moved like blood between her ribs.

Air and space began to bend around the swell of her and after walks she would lie on her back and fan herself to watch it shiver in rainbows.

Nora would sit in her beige linoleum kitchen and she would eat soup. Her long hair pulled back into a bun, her green housedress swarming out around her legs. She tapped her feet against the table legs and imagined the warm snake of movement in her belly as a fish with a baby's face and she laughed at it.

Her skin began to stretch and her abdominal muscles tore apart and her connective tissue turned to glue. Her round ligament sagged and pulled at her hip crests, paining her as she walked. Belly filled the living room and she no longer saw nor heard her feet shift across the rug and the noise was sometimes so deafening she would cling to her own ball shape like a hot balloon, until the panic exhaled and she would realize she was hovering, suspended several inches above the couch.

When she walked out on the street, the old man, the one with the hunched shoulders and the bent upper lip, would sometimes grab the tail of her skirt, which bellowed out beneath her now, from where he sat on the curb. And sometimes, she'd kick at his blue clawed hands and he'd only laugh and then shout nonsense at the girls playing dolls across the street.

She had had a feeling, like longing, since she was a little girl. But it wasn't emotion—it was physical, cousin to the noise that tied around her appendages like chain-link, but this was the sensation of space, like a shadow, or a cat, that hovered about her feet as if attached, but with motives and organs of its own.

When the baby was born, Nora was in the bathtub and first through her dilating cervix came a string. The doctor pulled and a few inches emerged, growing thicker into rope until it caught, as if wrapped around a table leg. The doctor told her not to push and she set fire in a ring. At last, I see a head, the doctor shouted. It is white and black. And the baby poured out in a tide of red seawater. It was made of newsprint and twine and it began to cry before the doctor smacked its bottom. With every birth, Nora told the doctor, the mind of God grows.

She swaddled the baby in a towel and when she was able to walk and the blood did not clot down her leg, she took it to the girls with their cradle on the corner and they dressed it in a pink gown and sang her rhymes from the letters on her cheeks. Nora brought her home and made her a hammock from a sheet. When the baby was seven months old, she walked out of Nora's front door and slid on her belly down the hall stairs to the street, where she fell in a puddle and dissolved into papier-mâché paste. The children picked up pieces of her and blew them in bubbles into the sky.

This time, with the men circled on the rug, Nora concentrated on the one with the soft hair most of all. She couldn't be alone with him, the sound would break her like glass across the side seam, but in the pillow of the pack, she loved him. This time, her belly grew wide and flat like an alligator's and her legs opened like jaws and this time a ball of fur rolled out into the doctor's bedside hands. Nora licked away the blood and fell asleep.

But the baby's eyes were closed and they never opened. When Nora woke and she pushed back the lids, the eyes were brown and dark with very little pupils.

In town, the man in the grocery shop made her a very small cardboard box and she tied it with a purple ribbon and buried it in a hole in the empty lot behind her building. When Nora was done, she went and sat on the streetside next to the stooped old man and he leaned his head on her shoulder. The noise grew very loud.

For the third baby, there was thunder. The doctor cackled like a crazy seaman against a storm and Nora's eyes rolled back and she nearly orgasmed and she nearly fell down. And when the doctor handed her the baby, rain was coming in the windows through a crack and Nora sucked the girl's furled earlobes and tiny toes.

The girl's hair grew long and golden as she nursed and she would curl her long legs around Nora's arm and ride her like a monkey and never unwrap, even to sleep, and never let go. Until one warm morning at thirteen months when she dropped to the ground and walked across the faded circle of rug on wobbly legs and Nora watched her as one watches an insect and was reminded of her own mother. Once, the girl turned and looked at her, and looked and looked into her eyes and it was like wind over the sea and quiet. She reached out and touched Nora's chin bone and a boil of water gathered there beneath the skin, then burst and the girl licked the salt from her fingers.

The man, the soft-haired one, sometimes came now to stay the night. He would sleep on the rug in the living room and she could hear his breathing and smell him from her bed.

There was tearing with the boys. There was ripping. The channel between her and the outside world was shredded. Maybe they had teeth, those boys. That's what the doctor said.

The boys were born together. Integument casing their two thoraxes where they met. One heart, the doctor said. Three lungs, he said. She lay in bed next to them, watching their chest rise and fall. The inhale of one became the exhale of another. One had black hair, one brown. Their heads faced toward one another and when their eyes were open they gazed into each other. They didn't look at Nora. It was difficult to feed them until she noticed that if she laid them upside down, four knees knocking against her chin, they could both latch on at once. She watched their tiny feet swim through the air, little toes lined up like rows of teeth. And her breasts would tingle and tighten in unison—jellyfish curling in their tails until it felt like bursting—and suddenly in a wave they'd unfurl, milk spurting into the babies' mouths and they'd squawk and swallow contentedly.

They spoke to each other. It was a language Nora couldn't understand but she could understand by the movements of their arms that they were speaking. Their arms, the ones closest to each other, would link or push apart in cadence with the babbles. Why they needed to speak, when they shared a body, she didn't quite know. They didn't share a brain and maybe that was it. The longhaired girl would lower her own face between them and hum. Then their arms were still, all four and they listened. Of course, it was only a few days. The doctor said they needed oxygen. That one of their lungs was filling with fluid and the two left would not sustain them. I'll have to cut them apart, the doctor said, and after, they lay there, mouths opening and closing like fish, and then, they went still. Nora, with red thread, hastily sewed them back together, blowing air between their gaping lips but of course, it was too late. The doctor carried them away in a white blanket made of fur.

Nora tried, again, but her canal was torn and the baby came out in pieces, too tiny to sew. After that, Nora was finished and she took a spoon and carved her uterus from where the webbing attached to her ilium. She boiled it into a stew and fed it to the scarved women in the street who giggled like girls and tongued the dripping from their wrists.

She tried tying the gold girl to her leg, to chase away that empty shadow there, but the girl would chew through the rope and roll around the apartment while she slept and anyway, Nora found the clamor had grown rather quiet.

After that, the girl walked everywhere and Nora watched her from the green chaise pulled close to the window in which she sat and never rose again.

Canal

The soap clung to her wrists, a dried film of tiny bubbles, the crackled layer a snake lifts scale by scale as it exits its skin. She stepped from her life, from her shoes and white dress and petticoat the way the snake shed his and she walked into the whiteness of the day. The sand rubbed beneath her toes. She pressed hard to scratch the balls of her feet and heels.

She had left the water running in the sink. It was spilling over now, soaking the rug and seeping so deeply into the floor that the rot of the boards would never heal and a year from now her husband's new wife's left leg would go right through to the knee. The babies were asleep in their cribs and when they woke, they would cry for two hours before Mirabelle returned from the commissary to prepare dinner.

She waded in the sea to her knees and sometimes dipped her hands to cool her neck, but she continued on in a straight line in the same unhurried pace of migrating animals.

Her brain was awash with ocean. Waves from an early afternoon tide splashed the brim of her mind. Two gulls flapped the blue distance of a thought. A hermit crab ticked its claws.

To her side the jungle forest opened in darkness. She was far from the Zone, long past any houses, any sign of human inhabitance. She sniffed. The deep, wet smell of life and death filled her chest; instinctively she crouched lower and crept, cat-like on two feet into the trail-less green.

The babies were quiet now, suckled in the brown arms of the women who did the caring for them. The husband had immediately sent for the Zone Police, who were busy interrogating the West Indians who lived at the base of the hill below, about whom the wives often complained of the smell and the noise. Three men were taken into custody. One man, spitting blood and several teeth onto the stained concrete floor, confessed. Three months later, he was hanged.

It was dark, sun or moon blocked by canopy. The ground was sparse by comparison, giving her room to make a path, but the air was engorged with noise. She began to recognize plants that Mirabelle had shown her and picked their leaves, chewing steadily as she walked. At last her eyelids and limbs, taut with unknown walking, grew round and limp. She climbed to the middle branches of a sickly-smelling mango tree, curled against the trunk and slept.

Eleanor had been twenty, ripe with their first child when her husband sent word that he'd acquired married housing and that she was to join him immediately. She hadn't wanted to go, despite her husband's, her President's admonitions that women were needed for their patriotic duty and that the Zone was utopia. But she'd heard of the women divorced on grounds of desertion, mostly through her husband's letters, so her mother packed her trunk and took her to the train station and Eleanor had gazed back at Louisiana with pain in her heart as the boat bobbed off toward Panama. Sick as a dog from pregnancy and the sea, she'd arrived nine days later to her husband's grand smile.

A thousand falls of a thousand hammers echo to the moon. Hands rustle in rock, where water seeps like time carving holes through stone.

Her skin pricked into goose bumps, hairs on end, frozen hunting dogs. It was morning, dawn in the dark forest and every muscle spoke of hunger. Kitchen, stove, already these words were draped in haze, like a dream just still grasped, like dynamite had been planted beneath her house and she'd walked out into a smoking wasteland where everything had been reduced to dust. And though the particles still floated around her mind, they could no longer coalesce into a single form she could wrap in image or name.

What she saw now were flower and fruit, leaf and twig and bug. A bird, one of hundreds in the canopy chorus, garbled above her and she watched her eyes telescope until she could see a bead of water roll across his tail feather and nothing else.

She fell back then, landing on her haunches in the moist dirt as a memory filled the lens and human noises clouded the air.

"Do you see him, Elle? Near the top, two or three branches down with the red stripe down his breast."

She couldn't.

"Yes, Papa, yes! I see him."

What filled her memory now was not the elusive black bird with the red stripe or the cold binoculars pressed hard against her eyes, the empty circle of nothing but row after row of green pine needle. What she remembered now was the overwhelming smell and feel of man as the girl in the picture nuzzled her blonde ringlets into the dark beard and furry chest of the father that held her aloft.

She pounced, and roughly chewed as feathers fell to her feet. The day filled with this. The days. Food filled the hours between sleep. With each death, each meal that carried her further toward survival, an image, a picture of a life she no longer knew, floated through the halls of her mind and out a door, into muscle or hair or blood, where they remained.

A ripping sound, tearing tendon shivers through Culebra Cut. Rock mountain and mud slide, set loose from solidity, and bury twenty-seven breathing men below.

Eleanor looked herself over in the mirror. She smiled. She beamed. The long white lace and pearls framing the curling blonde hair framing the lovely white skin, the lovely pink cheeks, the lovely pink lips, the lovely green eyes. She was lovely and it was her wedding. She beamed. Suddenly and unbidden, a fat tear rolled out her lovely eye and over the mound of lovely cheek, smearing a trail of powder in its wake. Eleanor dove her face into her kerchief while her mother and sister clucked around her, straightening hairs and preparing the bottles of powder and rouge. They repasted her face and she rose to meet her groom. Beaming, again.

It was two weeks before William returned to work. He sat, in the days before he went back to the cool engineering offices, in a rocking chair on the screened outdoor veranda, and looked past the yard cleared of brush that could harbor snakes, past their empty banana trees and the lime tree in blossom to the winding jungle, to green upon deeper green, and wondered about his wife. And he longed to hear her laugh. Mirabelle fixed his meals and left them on the silver platter beside his chair and he ate little between cigarettes and rum.

Iguana could not outrun her on an open branch. Birds were easily knocked aground.

Hercules pushes, his thirteenth thrust. Her limbs tear apart.

It was Christmas though it was muggy and hot as always. But a breeze blew in, cooling the house and perfuming it with the sweet blossoms from the lime tree and she'd invited Mr. and Mrs. Brecht, the Greenes with their three daughters, and several of the unattached young men from the offices for dinner. The commissary at Empire had stocked Christmas fixings like cranberries and mincemeat, which stood proudly in silver bowls on the long white tablecloth. She'd arranged for the turkey to be cooked in the monstrous ovens of the hospital, and everyone was awed as two of Mirabelle's sisters carried it, glossy and brown to the table. Voices sang throughout the rooms and the heartsick young men played chase with the children or flirted with the Greene girls and it felt, for a day, like home. Eleanor sat with the other wives in the parlor and listened to gossip about the latest ICC intervention between two wives of machinists who'd been steadily driving each other crazy with smart remarks and pranks.

"Well, she called ICC, tried to reach Goethals himself on account of Mrs. Nance had set loose a bat in her house," said Mrs. Brecht.

"A bat!"

"I'll say," said Mrs. Greene, "that I think it a sin that these women can occupy Mr. Goethals' valuable time with their petty roughneck foolery. There's a canal to be built here, and ladies should be ladies. Just shameful."

They nodded their heads and sipped lightly from their martini glasses.

"How did she know it was Mrs. Nance who'd set the bat loose?" asked Eleanor at last.

Mrs. Greene started in on an explanation but Eleanor's thoughts drifted and her ears picked up, across the hall, a conversation between her husband and one of the bachelor doctors.

"You'll find one soon enough, my boy, just make sure you're on the list for married housing. What about the oldest Greene over there, quite a fine young lady? And the nurses, why there must be dozens of them just looking for a husband."

She couldn't hear the muffled reply, but her husband's voice was confident and loud, slightly drunk and bounced easily across the room to her.

"Yes, yes, she's perfect. That's my Eleanor. Just perfect."

She ducked her head slightly and looked into her drink.

William went to dinner a month or so later, at Mrs. Greene's urging, at the house of a colleague. He ate voraciously for the first time since his wife's passing. Sarah Gayle was nineteen and fresh as a rose and she spoke to him kindly about the weather. Three weeks later they were married and she moved into the house.

Unforgiveness sparkles with salt. Tides take and give and fill the lacuna between legs. Unforgiveness licks lips with salt brine and open wide.

♦

The children rustle into the green. They are not allowed here, but Sarah Gayle is napping and Mirabelle is cooking and doesn't notice. Lily goes first, chasing a butterfly and William comes behind, younger, unsure. There is a trail beaten brown against the forest floor, the children follow. Lily pelts a rock at an iguana, Will hops like a frog, they trace the lines of a vine up a tree, climb a rock. There is movement in the bushes; they stop still, hairs on end. A woman emerges, smiling, she waves to them, they follow. She leads them to a hut made of trees, leaves hang across the roof, a mud stove smokes outside. She gives Lily a woven basket and gestures for her to open it. Inside are small brown balls, beans. Lily takes one out and, like the woman, rubs off the papery shell and puts it into her mouth. They are chalky and sweet and the children suck on them and laugh. The woman motions at the darkening sky and she takes the two children by the hand. She walks them far down the path, until they hear Mirabelle calling their names and they run toward her and when they look back the woman in the jungle is gone.

A conquering. Opening. An acquiescence to centrifugal force. A forcing. A letting. A manifesting. A destiny. Made manifest.

The legend goes that two teenaged boys, sons of American engineers, saw a female jaguar while hunting in the unknown jungle with a native boy as their guide. The cat, said the son who returned, was no regular jaguar. Her fur was deep yellow and spotted when they spied her from behind, reclining on a low branch. But as they moved closer, inching like snakes on their bellies and sniffing the husky scent of tropical dirt, she rolled on her back, revealing the most perfect set of ripe human breasts, pink nipples round and erect, and there between her splayed jaguar legs, a sweet, rounded, wet, and downy pussy. The boys froze on the ground. They couldn't move nor take their eyes from her. She looked at them with her jaguar eyes and, the boy said, arched her back and lay wider her legs.

At last his friend snickered, Fuck. He rose to his knees and began to crawl forward. The cat woman kept her gaze on him and didn't move, didn't even blink. The boy, the one on the ground still, his heart pounding, determined to be next.

The first boy was at the foot of the tree now, and wrapping his hands into the bark, he rose, slowly to his feet. The forest was dark as dusk, even in afternoon, but the jaguar's white breasts shone like moons as the boy reached his hand slowly, slowly to touch them. From the distance his friend and the native boy saw the cat stretch into a backbend and then they heard a purr. The boys on the ground pressed their own hardness into the dirt as he moved his hand down between the jaguar's legs and the leaves vibrated around them.

The legend veers into several versions at this point, depending mostly upon whether you're talking to whites or Panamanians or West Indians, but most involve the boy taking off his clothes, and then a flash of claws and teeth and fur.

"Two days later, the guide boy returned with his father and several uncles," Mirabelle says. She sits beside the stove with two of her neighbors, flapping dough against her palms. "They spent the night in the clearing of the tree with the low branch. At almost daybreak, at the deepest part of night, a female jaguar crept to the tree and stood before it on all fours. No one said anything about breast or cunt, but draped on her back, over her fur, they say, was the skin coat of a human, of a white man, sand brown hair and all."

Skinned

When she was finished stitching her own skin, the mother began on her daughter. She stretched the flesh taut over the wet structure of bones and gristle. The daughter moaned and squawked like a little bird, but she did not cry. The girl needed breath, the mother knew, so she went out into the pine trees, past the smoky edges of the town and filled herself with air. She returned, opened the child's mouth, and blew.

The girl's arm could not be saved. The mother mourned the memories stored there, read her daughter the stories written on each cell, before she buried it in the yard. On top of the fresh mound, a radish vine began to grow.

The soldiers had come in the night and left the town beneath a cloud of ash. Their jackals had sniffed her out below the floorboards and left her torn, the child's arm dangling in strips at her side. They were lucky though, that there was something to sew at all. Many people had begun to take animal hides or discarded plastic sheeting to cover their exposed meat. Not many people remained at all. The scout had spared them, she knew.

It was dark but his face had glinted silver with the moon and his eyes were melted onyx. They poured over her. He stood above her, breathing staggered, for a long time, the jackal snapping against its chain. Finally, he smiled at her, sharp, whittled teeth. She heard others charging behind him from the woods, heard walls being ripped apart, the bird-like screams—and in a crooked flash, time turning sideways, she saw his claw protract and lacerate the soft roll of her belly. Before her mouth could open to scream, he knocked her head against the floor and she was silent. She did not see him tear the girl's arm, or bundle the strips of meat inside the pouch across his chest.

The girl did not cry for her arm. It is still here, she told her mother. But the pulsating ghost space trailing her daughter was more than the mother could bear. She gave the girl tea to make her sleep and the mother removed her own arm at the shoulder, untied the stitched wound, and attached it to the girl. It helped sew itself onto the new body, and the mother found she still had some control of its movements, jerky and awkward though they were. For herself, she pulled the radish vine and inserted it between striated layers of muscle where it sprouted roots and began to grow.

Senna, the girl was called, and she was just like a seed from the beginning. Her hair was brown and curled around her round brown face, round brown eyes, small and squirrel-like and always watching.

To cross the world, the mother told Senna when she woke, we'll have to begin at daybreak.

They left their village burning behind them, the smell of singed hair all around. The fort on the hill was growing, tented skin walls blowing out in the wind, and from below it looked like it breathed and exhaled, expanding and shrinking in the haze of the rising sun. Senna opened her mouth against her mother's back, watching the mountains of vertebrae shift like a line of elephants under the skin. They rose and fell like the hills they walked and Senna laid her head against the sharp blade of her mother's shoulder and fell back asleep. Senna was tied to her mother with the vine and sometimes the leaves lifted to brush flies from her face. They were in the forest now, but the ground was hot, scorched, the trees blackened and wispy as hairs.

She smelled him before she saw him and without thought she felt Senna's arm, the one that had once been hers, move across her back to gently cover the girl's mouth. She dropped beside a pile of rocks at the base of a sandy hill and started to dig. Even with one hand she was swift and soon Senna was half buried. By the time he came over the ridge, only their faces were visible in the sand. He was coming from behind them. Her ears beneath the dirt, the mother could hear the earth creak against every footfall, she could feel him getting closer. Unable to turn her neck, she cranked her eyes back against her skull and she was able to make out movement and that was all. She closed them again. She could see him better that way. He was coming down the hill, almost straight for them.

If he had a jackal they had no chance, but she was fairly certain she heard only two feet. She could hear now the sand squeaking, felt the earth around her head shift. And the scent of decaying meat was almost unbearable. Then, silence in the ground.

She opened her eyes and again cocked them back as far as they would go. The hot white sky scraped her vision, and then there he was. He was nearly above them, perhaps a foot back. His hair hung greasy and unkempt from his head and elbows and scrotum. He was close enough that she could see the seams at his legs and underbelly where he'd been sewn. The stench made the water run from her mouth to her eyes and had her hands not been buried she wouldn't have been able to stop them from clenching her nose. He was fresh. The stolen flesh putrefying while his body absorbed it into its own. His milky blue eyes looked out, scanning the horizon, but the movements of his head told her that he saw very little. She watched a bead of sweat roll to the tip of his nose and hover, hang. She heard it splash onto the sand just inches from her face. She did not breathe. He closed his eyes and sniffed. A cloud rolled over the sun. The mother closed her eyes.

Then she heard his feet shift, lift and land. Lift and land again. She coiled further inside of herself like a snail and she felt the air of him blow past her. Then the footfalls were moving and by the time she exhaled, they were gone.

It took time to dig themselves out and when they were free the sun was much higher in the sky than she wanted and they had a long way to travel still before it set. At night, the mother knew, the skinned would fill these woods, spreading to farther and farther villages. They would be safer if they could make it beyond the forest. But at least the scout should be far away by now; he was young and alone and out in the middle of day, unpredictable and likely hungry.

Senna walked now, bouncing in her childhood gait. The long arm worried after her, dragging almost, hesitant. The trees grew thicker and denser again, pine needles stretching to reach one another across empty space, and Senna gathered the fallen ones and laid them on her head in a thorny crown and her one motherhand wove them into a cloth as she walked. The sun was creeping down, the air cooling like navy and she draped the cloak over her shoulders. The mother noticed a notch in the bark of one tree, and a few hundred feet later, another, and knew it was a trail. They followed it for several hours and the light was almost gone when they buried themselves for the night.

♦

The trees were growing shorter, their branches warping into knots, their leaves tight and brushy. The light a haze. Senna was walking. Never out of reach of the radish vine, which hovered close behind, ready to grab her neck at any rustle it seemed. Senna draped the pine needle cloth over her head to block out the sun. Her feet dragged in the sandy soil. A wasp landed on her forearm. It was sleepy. Lethargic maybe from the heat. It let her close her palm above it, allowed her to trap it there. She cupped it into her hand. She held it, carried it as they walked, sometimes feeling its small wings bat against her palm. Sometimes its stinger scratching gently like a fingernail. In a few hours, it was still. She tore a small hole in the seam of her dress and nested its body there.

Suddenly, the mother dropped to her knees, the vine cuffed Senna's foot mid-step and yanked back, knocking the girl flat to her belly on the red sand. Her motherarm swept to the girl's mouth and pinched it shut. She dropped to the ground next to her daughter. They were in near-desert now, there were few places to hide but the mother's eyes scanned quickly—scattered brush, it would do. She lifted her nose, sniffing intently, trying to be sure. She smelled nothing strange. Nothing new. She tried to still her breath, listening deep. Quiet. But lights, out on the dunes, they flickered. Her head peeked up, watched the streaks reaching up into the stark blue. They lay there a long time. No sound. No smell. The lights still there. Finally, the mother decided to move closer; it was a risk, but what else was there to do. Anywhere they walked they would be seen. When they got close enough, she could see that whatever made the light was lying on the ground. It could be something buried. Someone. But perhaps not. Finally they could see objects, scattered. Still no sign of anything, anyone. They walked up the dune. Broken shards and long white bones, stripped dry and baked over many weeks, months. Pieces of cracked mirror. The mother leaned over, saw her weathered face in strips against the sand, a blue-sky halo. She shut her eyes and turned away. It had been many, many years. Senna lifted a triangle of mirror and slipped it into the pocket of her dress. The mother dug a hole. She pieced the skeleton together as best she could. It was young, but not a child. A boy most likely. Narrow hips. Several hand bones were missing, the teeth from his skull and the whole bottom jaw bone, the rail of his shin. When the parts were all arranged, Senna came from where she'd been twirling down the hill and together they covered him in sand.

There was a shock of cold light, like water, alongside them sometimes now, and the mother knew they were getting close and that her own mother had come to walk with them. Senna danced around the whispery shadow, chased it and laughed. They stopped to eat, huddled together in the sparse shade of a thorn tree. The mother rested, for just a short while, she said, and while her eyes were closed, Senna angled her back to her. She nodded her head aside, to make sure her mother was asleep, and pulled the glass from where she'd woven it into the crevasses of her cloak. Slowly, breath strained, she lifted it before her face. The round chin, the mound of lip, the empty recesses of her nose. She gazed into the eyes that met her. Her mother began to stir and Senna slipped the mirror back between the needles.

♦

It was growing late and they would have to find a place to sleep for the night. The mother saw an outcropping of rocks in the distance and knew it would both be shelter and danger. She also knew they would not reach it before dark. But what choice did they have. The sun set and Senna climbed onto her back and was soon asleep. The desert cold dropping over their heads now.

Then, something in the pit of her stomach turned. The mother froze, the toes of one foot barely lifted off the ground, mid-step. No, no, no. They were half a mile, maybe, from the rocks. How had she not smelled it earlier? Heard something? It was heavy in the air suddenly, sulfur and decay. More than one, she thought. A group. Three at least. She lowered slowly to the ground. It was near full dark now. Twilight seeping blue. They would be out soon, she knew. At night, they roam. Burrow? she asked the flickering blue shape that hovered beside her again. Run? They will have jackals, the mother answered herself. It won't be long. Senna rustled on her back, her sweet sleep breath rolling across the mother's neck, ear. The mother moved swiftly. She pulled all the food from her pack and tossed it to her side as far as she could. She crept, hands and feet, Senna clutching in her sleep to her mother's humped back, in the opposite direction. She buried the girl deep, only her mouth and nose above ground. The mother wound the rope around her wrist in a loose knot and gripped the knife in her palm. She smelled blood. Coppery and sickly sweet. Something fresh. The jackals would be sated. And the men. The only reason they hadn't smelled her yet.

She ran, all fours, to the crop of rocks. Two, three. She sniffed deeply as she ran. Only one jackal, she thought. Then her mind grew quiet, wide as the desert. As she approached the rocks, she lifted to two feet and grabbed a large stone in the vine. The jackal screeched. The rustling of bodies—leaping, spinning, reaching for weapons. Sliding around the rock, she saw the first scout just before her, back turned. She hammered the rock down against the high point of his skull, barely registered the slick crunch as he crumpled.

Two others and the jackal, ripping against his leash tied between the rocks. One scout reached for her, lunged, his hand wet and dark. She slashed at his arm with the knife, hitting a place where the bone must not yet have set and tearing it in two like a cloth. It dropped to the ground. His other hand though, closed in on her neck and squeezed as she flung the knife, all the strength in her arm, against his chest. It bounced back against something hard, then found purchase between two ribs. He gasped, blood oozing from his mouth, but still he squeezed and his claws on the back of his hair-covered knuckles extended and lashed into her chin, and she felt two more arms wrap her from behind. The stone rose and cracked down against the side of his skull. Both eyes bulged left, looked like they might exit their sockets, and then went blank. He dropped to the sandy floor.

But she was held tight now. The scout behind her kicked out her knees and dropped on top of her on the ground, and with one hand yanked the vine from her shoulder. She howled as the roots ripped out, cloaked in white tendon and gristle. Knees on her back, her face and arm pinned to the ground, she heard the man pause, before he crashed the rock down on her hand, and she heard the crack splatter and felt nothing and watched her arm go flat and limp. He rolled her over and the knife rolled from her grasp and onto the sand. She heard the jackal again, gnarled teeth batting against each other and a frothy snarl straining against the rusted metal chain. The scout ripped the rock from the vine and tossed it at the animal, smarting him in the nose, and he whimpered and went quiet. He looked down at her then, the scout, but his eyes jumped left and right, unable to steady and focus. She struggled but he gripped her tight. He moved his hands to her face, rubbed across her forehead, over her eyes and mouth, inserted his finger against her tongue. He laughed. Dragged his hand through the blood now dripping from the underbelly of her chin, he lifted his fingers to his mouth, and sucked. He rubbed his hands down her chest, over her breasts, squeezing hard at the nipples, down her stomach, between her legs. His mouth opened in a grunt, sharpened teeth caught in moonlight.

The jackal jumped up, hissed low and deep, nearly wrested free from the chain but snapped back instead against the rock. The skinned scrambled to rise to his feet but it was too late. Blood shot from his neck, black, out into the dark night like a rising spring. Senna stood behind him. Sand in her hair. The sharp shard of mirror, stained, in her small hand. Her eyes wide with night. But before he fell to his side, liquid pooling underneath him, his claws shot out, like reflex, and tore into the soft flesh of the mother.

In the Blue

"I'll tell you a story," she says, and then she says, "God is a woman in the desert."

She is sitting in the blue chair in the corner. I can't see her, really, in the dark. And this isn't the story she was telling, this one about God, but she loses her train of thought often now. Words, like the spit dribbling down her chin, wipe away sometimes and leave just the shiny film behind. The story she was telling, the one she lost, is the one of her childhood, of immigrating, of her small nose pressed tight against the American glass, watching the train in a store's Christmas display. And it is the story she was telling me when she died. Not when she actually died. We were watching penguins on TV then. Not at the moment she died then, but the last time she was conscious. Earlier that day. Before the cough started.

She starts coughing now and I wonder if it's because I was thinking about it. I wonder if that's how this works. I don't know how this works. She asks for water and I bring her a glass and put it on the windowsill next to the chair. I'd say she smiles, but that would presume she had a mouth. I'd say she drinks the water, but that would presuppose that mouth that I cannot confirm. Or disconfirm. But she wets herself, and the blue chair, and the smell of urine is impossible to deny. I scrub the chair while she sits on the floor, rocking and ducking her face. Then, she is back in the chair, and I am back in bed. Trying to sleep but she is still talking.

"It is cold and she is walking and the wind blows the sand right through her."

"That's not what you said, Ma. That's not what you were saying," I say and I am surprised at my anger.

"Oh," she says and she's quiet now. I see her head nodding back and forth, like it's chasing something.

The train, I almost tell her.

I think I fall asleep, but I hear her again and she's laughing.

"Look, Pa, look! Smoke! See the lights in the little town. Where are the people, the tiny people who live in there?"

She is standing. Her hands pressed against the window, her nightdress swinging out behind her.

"Mom," I say. She doesn't turn. Doesn't flinch. "Ma, come away from the window. Come to bed." She spins and looks at me, if you can call it that—she is looking at me but she's looking through me too, and her face, it is like a child's.

She curls in bed next to me; she's warm and vibrates a little when she breathes.

In the morning, I'm working in the kitchen and she's humming all around. I catch her reflection in my screen and I watch her. She's standing in front of the fridge, looking at the photos, the wedding invitations, last year's Christmas cards. Her hair is silver, which it never was, and long, thinning at the bottom in broken wisps. Her body is bent; it still crooks to the right like it always did, but more so now, and it curves forward in a ricketed way it never did when she was alive. I strain to see her hand, the left one, to see if the ring finger is missing from her accident, and when I see it, wrapped at its stump in shiny scarred shell, it's like someone punched me in the stomach and I lose my breath. I close the computer and lay my face against the cool case. I feel her fingers in my hair and when I wake up, it's braided like a girl's.

I make her soup for lunch and leave it next to the blue chair.

I walk to the corner for cigarettes. I shouldn't leave her alone for long, but I cannot bear the thought of my apartment. I sit on the park bench and watch a child repeatedly try and fail to walk backward up a slide. I watch an old couple try to wipe crumbs off each other's face. I am sick and I walk to get coffee and a bag of chips.

I get home, and I know it's been too long, and there are dishes all over the floor. Bowls in a circular pattern around the living room rug, skirted by plates along the fringes. I nudge them aside with my foot as I make my way to the kitchen. Mugs in a line; the one I made in art class in fifth grade, with the alligator head and the chip at the mouth, waiting at the front. Glasses across the counters. And it's quiet.

"Ma!" I yell. I don't mean to. Don't want to. But I yell.

Something breaks in my bedroom. I hear the breaking sound.

The bowl is in pieces on the floor, floating in soup. She is looking down at it in confusion. She looks at me and she shrinks under my eyes. "I'm so sorry," she says, and she starts to cry. I tell her it's okay. Tell her to lie down and I mop the soup up with a shirt from the hamper.

"I cleaned for you," she says from under the covers. "I wanted to clean the house for you. You work so hard." I don't say anything. And then she is snoring.

♦

I looked at a stack of pictures of her the other day. They were all of the last few years. As I flipped through, her hair got shorter, thread-like and sparse, her face got thinner with each one, but when I got to the last couple it made me jump a little—the whole structure of her bones changed, her eyes were drooped and hollow, more socket than eye, and it was like you could see right through her skin. I flipped through the pile quickly, like an animation. This is kind of what it's like to look at her now.

I help her change her clothes. She sits on the edge of the bed and lifts her arms high as she can. Underneath she is a web of blue veins and mounds of flesh. Her breasts fall like worn shopping bags down her chest and rustle when she breathes. I pull a clean nightdress over her head and pluck the hairs that have dropped on the bed.

She's asked me to put on old family movies, so I dragged out the tub of VHS and the VCR and now she is on the floor in the living room, smiling, in her flickering way. She's ashy and flaking, so I rub lotion on her limbs and then I tie her hair into a bun.

The day my mom died, I asked her what I was like as a child. She told me I lied a lot, to get myself out of trouble. I was putting lotion on her and I was trying not to look at the way the skin hung off, rubbery and loose. I was trying not to look at the distinct lines where the cells cross each other, how deep those lines had become, like I could stick my fingernails in and pull her apart. It was making me nauseous, and I was trying not to look.

On the TV is a scene from my eleventh birthday. She is fussing over a big cake, bringing it to the table. It's white with blue trim frosting and it was beautiful and I remember it. I blow out the candles, and this isn't what she wants, I didn't wait for the song and now she is yelling at me and now the screen goes dark.

She looks up at me now, from the floor, and gives me a crooked smile.

"The woman in the desert," she starts again, pulling herself from my dance recital on the screen, "is digging for bones." Stories recur all the time. The one of the Christmas train, for example, she tells nearly every day. But still. So I indulge her. And because, maybe, she would know.

"Why bones, Ma? Why would God want bones?"

But she only starts humming and watching me, twelve, dance.

I stopped seeing Ben when she started showing up. We were in bed that first night, me draped in his arms, him grazing his hand through my pubic hair. His soft hands, soft from soft work, she used to say. She never liked Ben; she thought he'd never grow up. Which is exactly why I chose him, of course. She'd huff under her breath when he came over for dinner. And the blankets were on the floor. Us naked in the streetlight. And my eyes closed and opened. And I saw her shape in the blue chair. I thought it was clothes and as I tried to refocus she got up and moved toward the bed. She stood over us, the image of her kind of shaking at the edges, and she didn't cluck her mouth or huff, she just smiled. I didn't try to tell him why. I just stopped calling him back.

I've been out on the fire escape, pretending not to smoke. I hear a little scream and I cut myself going back in through the window. When I get there she is sitting on the blue chair, her face is red and her eyes wide, more eye than socket. She doesn't say anything, and I smell it.

Finally: "I think I had an accident," she murmurs.

Body or not, the shit stains are real and I curse and yell out phrases like "what the hell is wrong with you?" and "why are you doing this to me?" as I try to scrub them out of the chair. I see her in the reflection of the window, curled in the corner, rocking and shaking her head and maybe she is crying.

I leave her in the corner. Brown spots on her ass under her bent-up legs. Her hair a tangled mess. I go to the bar. It's just starting to get dark and I will stay here all night. I drink Jameson on the rocks, one after another, and watch water drops gather and run down the side of the glass. There are blue and red lights in the air and a man down the bar is looking at me.

Now he's walking me home, the sidewalk broken and shifty under my feet. His hands on my elbows, my back, my breasts. We stumble up the stairs and in through the door. I don't trip over anything and I drag him across the room. I fall back into the blue chair and pull him by his belt loops in front of me. I take him in my mouth with my eyes opened wide. There is a flutter in the corner, a flash of light and I suck harder, push him against my throat. I stand up and turn around; he lifts my skirt and pushes inside of me from behind.

The dawn is coming in the window, the light that pre-color gray and I see myself, my breasts bouncing to his thrusts, lifted and tight, then long and stretched, like hers. Next to me, her reflection. I don't know what her face is doing, but she's standing there, pointed in my direction. I reach back and rip my boot off. I throw it at the window and it cracks, spiderwebbing her into fractured pieces. She doesn't move.

"Get out," I say. "Get the fuck out."

He slows for a second, starts to mumble.

"Fuck me," I say and rock back into him. "And you, you get out."

He slams against me, several more times, then moans, hard, shakes, and pulls away.

I look at my broken self, a nipple kaleidoscoped, an eye sliced in two. The morning is brightening, bluing the room. There is nothing behind me but a doorway.

"Ma?"

I hear him close the door.

"Ma, what does she want with the bones?"

Your Small Hummingbird Hands

There was the curve of his neck. Chin, turned to the side. Cheek, laid against the seat. There was the street-lamp yellow painted across his face in rectangles, sucked up suddenly into black and gray and you had to turn around to look at the road. There was the smell of him, even from the front seat, a smell of sticky, of dirt, but mostly new, like an unused car or an unborn baby. There was a feeling, and it was inside of you but it felt like it was the whole car that wanted to swallow him just like that with the buckles across his chest and his hummingbird bone hands, with a straw, into your cavity and let him grow there again. There was a feeling that felt like it was the air circulating the car that wanted to climb back into the seat and climb your flesh inside his and grow in a ball from his belly button, or maybe just lay your skin on top of his quietly like a thin, unshaggy fur.

It reminded you, do you remember? of those days when the color was very vivid and fresh and every bad thing felt good. It reminded you of that feeling when life gets so thick and something pushes, hard, against that veil that holds out what is life from what is not. It reminded you of that feeling that you had not had for years, of life bearing down on you, not like a weight, not like now, but like air on a humid black night laying heavy soft on your body like it touched you, like life was rubbing your arms and all your hair stood on end from the electricity of it.

There was the streetlamp yellow and the skin of his neck, sticky, and a hummingbird breath beating in his nose. It reminded you, not the yellow or the skin or the breath, but the feeling that now filled the car, of his lips and the heaving and the taste like lime. It reminded you of that time when every bad thing was good and his hands on your stomach and smoke hanging in the air and the air so thick you could write your name in it and burn a tear right through to where the things that were not life floated.

You pulled his hands across your stomach and you trembled.

There was streetlamp yellow and bass and dirt on your bare feet. There was black you think now you could only imagine, that it never existed but it did. There were stars that white too. There was air laying heavy and wet on your skin like a furless coat. There were hands, big hands raking your stomach. And smoke and your name hanging in the air. There was a humming bass but it started at the pit of your pelvis and snaked up, the vibration, around your ribs and over your sternum as his big hands raked and the air rubbed and life pressed hard against you.

There was the breath, hummingbird wings beating against his nose, fragile and violent together, and the breath, the sticky humidity of it, the fragile violence of it, reminded you, in the space of a moving car, of the weight of the air like life leaning into you, pushing into, raking across your stomach.

There was night, it was always night, the black so black it must be memory and the stars white white and all around in the air birds were flying. There was noise, so much bass vibrating, the crickets and the frogs pulsing, like this must be the humming sound of life that pressed so hard up against the screen that tried to hold it in. There were lips wet with lime and smoke hanging your name in the air. The air fresh like a peach, like you'd never felt air before, like it was your first time and every bad thing still so good.

There was black night and so much room in the sky and all there was was big hands raking across your stomach and life pressing hard against you. Do you remember? That life pressed so hard that what was on the other side disappeared and there were no hummingbird bones and graywhite skin. And with his big hands raking your stomach, there was no she.

There was streetlamp yellow. There was dirt on your feet. There was vibrating air. And there was no she, she who wrapped you in casing, she who had held back all that was not life with her big crooked hands, she who was hummingbird bones and skin—there was no she. And every bad thing still good in yellow, in raking hands, in black black heavy night.

There was yellow. Black rectangles. There was a road you had to turn to look at. Buckles across his chest. Sticky dirt breath and a hummingbird beating inside his nose. There was a car. Moving in space and a night, more purple than black. There was a feeling that reminded you. That slipped like air, thin and high like a soprano note through a crack in the window. A chin, laid against a seat. A curved neck. And you tried, with small bent hands to hold back all that was not life that pressed against the veil and threatened to tear like a name in the night.

There was the curve of the neck. Cheek, laid against a pillow. Chin, dropped open, mouth gaping a black so black it must be memory. Breath, falling, like dropping wings. Small crooked hands, hummingbird bones draped in a graywhite furless coat. Holding back nothing that seeped through screen.

But in night black black and stars white and hands big and raking and vibrating from your center to a place in your mouth where it melted—there was only that. There was only your name hanging in smoke in a tear in the sky and life and not life seeping through and melting in your small hummingbird hands.

You pulled his hands across your stomach, and you trembled.

Birth [in Reverse]

I had someone turn me inside out once. Did you ever have one of those? There are many ways to be turned in reverse.[1, 2, 3, 4, 5]

The problem, of course, is getting right side out again. As if there was a right side. But skin on the outside, that seems to be useful, regardless.

---

1. Giving birth. Then I understood the cleaving open. Then it was like someone grabbed each labia, and slowly, not fast, but like an undialing speculum, wrenched my ilium apart. And out came pouring with blood and seawater and baby, my insides.

2. Watching someone die. When you die and your breath leaves, it pulls the insides out with it and the body is no longer a self but an empty meatsack, which soon begins to rot. And when you watch that process happen to someone else, a little of you is torn out too. Autolysis begins immediately. You start to digest yourself. You putrefy.

3. Walking away from each other. The baby, the boy, crying between you. Divorce, marriage, these are not the important pieces, what I mean is: losing the life you thought was yours. How did I describe this one: I was a bombed out building. You know the pictures, where you can see the walls torn away, an office with the desk against the wall, phone still in place waiting to ring, a filing cabinet left partway ajar. And beneath, the beams like broken bones poking out of the limen, the plaster tearing away into rubble like a zombie-ripped stomach and you, watching the intestines slowly tumble out.

Women are snakes.[6] Ouroboros ate her own tail, after all.

1

I was looking at a chart on the wall at the doctor's office. There were three clear plastic layers you could lift up, over the outlined human body, each depicting a different system: the blood, the nerves, the lymph. I looked at the snaking roads traversing our bodies, the hatch marks and chicken scratch and realized it was a language, and I read words in there. Though I couldn't translate them, and now I've forgotten what they were. I need to carry a pen. At home, I tried tracing the lines down my appendages with a pen. Then, I took a bath and as the ink filled the tub, I felt the water sog my boundaries, felt my organs seep into the liquid until the bathtub itself was my body and I could see it stretch as I inhaled.

---

4. Betrayal. This is the one I was referring to in the first place. This one resists a gerund. Being betrayed? Being deceived? Someone (a lover, partner) undermining your reality? Being lied to, day in and out, year after year. Convinced that what you perceive and feel is wrong, that who and what you are have been misnomers all along. This one, when someone gets under your skin and then slowly, like you hardly even notice, turns it around until suddenly you look down and your circulatory system and all your nerves are on the outside and you wonder why every breeze burns. But we don't have to wait for someone to do this to us. It was not unfamiliar. We are women, after all.

5. Adolescence: puberty, ecdysis, what have you. Becoming a woman.

6. And the serpent said, come, my child, and the serpent said, eat. And the god with no face said, you shalt not eat. And the no-face god said, you shalt die. And the serpent said, eat and you will know everything and you will swallow the god of no face again, and woman took a bite of her fingers and ingested her own hand.

♦

My baby was born in the tub and he was a fish, swimming up to meet me, tied to me by a string of pearls. Out next came his doppelgänger. This is your shadow, I told the boy. You will encounter him in the future and you will kill him, or you will be killed. The shadow-self shriveled and buried itself in the dirt to make a shell, for when they would meet again. I should have eaten him, but he slithered away. I feed my son eggshells to make him strong.

He looked like me, my baby, but then his feathers filled in and his flesh darkened and he told me, I am not you.

2

Naked mole rats do not live like mammals but like insects. Their social structures are closer to those of bees and ants, that is. They carve elaborate tunnels beneath the ground. There is a queen, and she rules. And she is larger than the rest, she is enormous. Every day she grows. She stretches space between her vertebrae and gets longer. The naked mole rat queen is the only animal in the burrow who reproduces. She secretes a message in her urine that tells the other rats not to breed, and they listen. And when she dies, the colony will revolt, until another naked mole rat expands in size, grows spaces in her spine—until she becomes queen.[7]

My mother died and when she came back to haunt me I hated her smell.

---

7. The colony revolts. The insects wandering my internal psychic labyrinth bite at each other and claw blindly. Pulling at the limits of the body, stretching gaps in the axial skeleton, stretching gaps to fill empty space.

3

I stood in front of the mirror looking at my flesh as it changed. If I stood all day, maybe one week, I thought, I can see it change. I marked my body as a child, to make sure it grew. I made an X with blue marker. When this X is on my breast, not just beside it, I said, I will know that I have breasts. I did this now, as an adult. When my back is flat against the wall, and I can see the mark on my navel, sticking out from below my breasts, I will know that I am pregnant.

When I slept is when I grew, though, so I tried to keep my eyes open in the night. I developed night vision and X-ray vision too, to see the spaces open between my bones.

I forgot to draw an X in the air between us though, and one day when I looked we'd grown so far that he wasn't in the frame at all.[8]

I tried to fit back into my bed but my neck was too long and my head just dangled loosely at its end.

4

The coming undone—it has to happen in steps, of course, like a frog in a pot as the water slowly boils.[9]

I said, I am cold and he said, you are not cold. It is warm, how silly to think you are cold in air like this. I glued fur and scales over my meat, and I shivered beneath them. You are not cold, you are not cold, you are not cold, I told myself, to the clacking of teeth against bone.[10]

---

8. This is the scene where your life walks away.

9. The who and the when of betrayal don't matter anymore. What matters is that he made me override my cells. Doubt my skin.

10. The problem, of course, is that I'd been doing this since I was a child.

I lift the plastic flaps and examine each system under my sheathing. The brown arteries, the gray of my nerves, lymph nodes. I feel him brush by, and I shudder.

I wrote my name all over my body, *nora nora nora* in ink after he was gone.

5

Hormonal changes cause the epidermis to increase protein synthesis and apolysis occurs, a separating of the epidermis from the old endocuticle. Into the empty space, cells secrete molting fluid, which digests the outgrown cuticle. Proteins and fat travel through pore canals to create new laminae of concrete and wax.[11] Contractions of muscles and an intake of air cause ecdysis, crack the exoskeleton along its sutures and out crawls a teneral, pale and unhardened.[12]

11. The point, isn't it, is that the thin membrane which separates inside from outside, me from you, is an illusion, isn't it. Its literal structure flaking and dying and falling away, second by second, as I write this. Its metaphorical structure opening in porous fashion, sieving through whatever I believe is small enough to pass.

12. And woman, standing in the garden, pulled open the lips of her vagina, the origin of the world, turning the body inward out, and made a new skin.

Eyes [Un]Closed

She builds houses from their bones. It is cold cold and dark and the wind tears sand through the air as if it is sieved, and she is walking. There are voices under the wind, under the sand, and she is following. There are stars—holes in the sky—but they give no light.

There are crabs in the desert and holes in the sand but the crabs don't burrow. They carry rocks on their backs and fold inside when the wind blows hard. They are unlike crabs. They are unlike turtles. They don't crawl into their rocks; they collapse underneath. She lifts one from the sand. Its head snaps up. Its face painted white with a red mouth, red rims around the eyes, snaking red hair. A black tongue moves out of the mouth, between sharp teeth and a hiss. It reaches its neck and snaps at her. She puts her finger behind the mouth and onto the hind legs. The legs are skeletal with smooth, amphibious scales. She rubs them gently. The crab ceases its hiss. It curls its legs. It hums. She looks at the face. Past the streaked red and white paint, the black gaping tongue. Its eyes are moistened and round. Its eyes are elephant eyes and full of time.

She tosses the rock in her basket. She gathers more, each with the same face to carry home and boil for soup. The bones hum under the sand and she is following. The wind doesn't stop and she has far to go. The rocks rattle in her basket. The crabs hiss.

The ground shakes as she passes and her salted hair trails behind, carving rivets in the sand. Sometimes she stops and with a broom brushes the sand aside. Sometimes she stops and digs. Her basket is empty, except for the crabs. The bones hum and she follows. There are blackbirds that look green against the night. They swoop down sometimes and steal strands of her hair. They lift them into the air and web the world. She walks, she drags her feet and the ground wobbles. The birds gather crabs. They carry them into the air in their beaks and rip off their heads and legs with their tongues. They drop the rocks to the ground. The ground shakes. The ground breaks into holes. She must mind the falling rocks. She must mind the holes. Her hair drags behind her and fills the holes. Sometimes in the holes, there are bones.

She stops and sniffs. She spins in a circle and her hair nests at her feet. Then, she begins to dig. Her nails are long and looped and yellowed. They are hard and they dig into the sand and they dig a hole much bigger, much deeper than the holes the birds make with rocks. It is unlike a hole. It is a cavern. She sniffs and she continues to dig. She digs feverishly now and the sand is humming and so is she. Grains of sand pile behind her in a mountain and the birds caw and drop rocks from the sky and she digs. She stops now. She has found it. The bone is white against the white sand and littered with holes. She rises and spins in a circle and her hair loops the hole and she kneels. She spits over the bone. The cave fills with water and the bone floats up to her. She takes it. She licks it and puts it in her basket. She has a bone.

Further along, she stops and sweeps aside sand with her hair. Another bone, white and socketed appears. She drops it in her bucket.

She walks. There is a bird on the ground. A bird that fell. It is unlike a bird. It is a fallen bird and broken. The worms that live under the sand will smell it and come for it soon. Its feathers green on the sand. Its blood black and seeping. Its eyes open and going back years and years. Its eyes are full of bones. She lifts the bird and puts it in her basket. She wipes the sand with her hair and smashes a crab's head between her fingers and leaves it for the worms.

She must return soon. Her grandson must be hungry. She hears a humming and she walks on. Walks away from the bird where it lay and away from the hungry child. She walks. The sand rends holes in her skin. The birds sometimes lower, sometimes fly down and rip small bits of flesh with their beaks and lacerate the web of her and the wind whistles through.

She comes to a place she knows but she's never been. Rocks sit circled and she crosses through the middle. She kneels, swallows nightbreath into her lungs and blows. Sand scatters. Under the sand is more sand and under the sand is mud and in the mud are bones. She digs deeply and finds her, bones caked still in milky skin, and humming.

The grandmother pulls her, pulls the bones in a body from the hole, pulls the limbs out like a starfish. Arranges the corpse, a cross in the sand. With her teeth, she bites along the hem of derma; the cuticle splits at the top of the head, rives down the neck and spine. Inside, white gelatin pulsates. She flays the flesh, peels it off in threads. She uncrosses the wires of vessels, uproots the organs one by one. She cracks the skull, cuts the dura and extracts the pulsing brain, a worm curled in on itself, a crab plucked from its shell. Unraveling the infinite loops, she stretches the spiderweb over the sand, steps carefully through the empty spaces, marks holes like stars in the sky. She stands the bones in the sand, guards at the entrances to the labyrinth. Perched in the center—organs around her in a nest, heart trembling at her feet—she tears teeth into her own palm and red rushes to the surface. Before it drips she presses her hand against the heart and holds it there.

The wind blows fierce across the desert, slashes at the old woman's loose pelt. It swirls around her now, around the organs and bones and neural web and raises them into the air, spinning them at her ankles. Sucking the body pieces in a cyclone, up and into the opening whorl of her now, up into her vagina and up into her cervix and up into her uterus and colliding there, back into a shape. Curled into itself, a snail. The chorion grows around it like a skin. Her eyes remain unclosed. She wrenches the eyeballs from her skull, claws the voice from her throat. She calls its name. Time stands tiptoe on the precipice, on the brink of erasure. Against her womb, a heart beats.

Acknowledgments

Thank you to Kian, my reason for everything, always. Thank you to my family, for their unfailing love and support. To my dad, David Morgan for his faith and support through it all; to Kristin Morgan and Lauren Lauritano for being such important parts of my formation and growth, from then to now; and to my mom, Linda Morgan, whose memory, loss and love is scattered throughout this book and throughout my days.

Thank you to Elisabeth Sheffield, for believing in me and this book, and for her guidance, encouragement and support every step along the way. Thank you to Jeffrey DeShell, for pushing me and this collection to be better. Thank you to Marcia Douglas, for knowing this would be a book, and being a guiding, supportive presence throughout my writing career. Thank you to Stephen Graham Jones, for motivation to play with narrative and genre.

Thank you to *Pleiades Magazine* for publishing a version of the story, "A Wing Unfolds in the Dark." Thank you to the Center for the American West for publishing and awarding the Thompson Award to a version of the story "Motherless."

Thanks to my friends and colleagues at CU Boulder, and especially my MFA cohort for patiently reading and giving excellent feedback to many incarnations of this book along the way, and just for general badassery and for a wild ride. Thanks to Marcie Cole and Annalise Sorensen, whose belief in me no matter what is sometimes shattering. Thank you to Mariesa Ho and Xavier Gitiaux, et al, for housing me, feeding me and being my family. Thank you to all of my students; I'm not sure you really know how much I love you guys.

Thank you to all of the authors who inspire me, for motivation, guidance and the dream. Thank you to the muses.